CW00913543

RUN
TO THE
WESTERN
SHORE

ALSO BY TIM PEARS

In the Place of Fallen Leaves

In a Land of Plenty

A Revolution of the Sun

Wake Up

Blenheim Orchard

Landed

Disputed Land

In the Light of Morning

The Horseman

The Wanderers

The Redeemed

Chemistry and Other Stories

RUN
TO THE
WESTERN
SHORE

TIM PEARS

Swift

SWIFT PRESS

First published in Great Britain by Swift Press 2023

1 3 5 7 9 8 6 4 2

Copyright © Tim Pears 2023

The right of Tim Pears to be identified as the Author of this Work has been
asserted in accordance with the Copyright, Designs and Patents Act 1988.

Typesetting and text design by Tetragon
Printed and bound in Great Britain by CPI Group (UK) Ltd, Croydon, CR0 4YY

A CIP catalogue record for this book is available from the British Library

ISBN: 9781800752979
eISBN: 9781800752986

For Rory and Miranda

1

H<small>E</small> could hear the barbarians coming from a long way off, a discordant cacophony. Tuneless trumpets blaring, drums thumping all out of rhythm. He could hear them splashing across the river at the horse ford, Hen Domen, and he could hear them coming up from the ford. Then one after another the drums and trumpets stopped. It was as if a signal for them to cease the racket had been given but each drummer and trumpeter only noticed the order at random. A raucous rabble.

He heard the scuff and scumble of the horses' hooves on the dry turf now, the clinking of harness. Then he saw them coming up from the river, at first only the tips of their spears over the brow of the slope, then the plumes on their helmets, and gradually their forms entire, horses and riders, rising.

A lone figure came cantering past this cohort and trotted into the camp at their head. His helmet hung on one

of the rear horns or pommels of his saddle. He wore chequered trousers, leather boots, a red silk tunic beneath a
shirt of iron ring mail. He had a gold torc around his neck.
His only weapon was a long sword, in a bronze scabbard
attached to a belt of metal loops, worn on his left side.
The dark horse he rode was abnormally large for these
people of the hill country. A mare perhaps fifteen hands
high, the horse had well-muscled, compact shoulders. She
had a long, arched neck and a beautiful small head, with
eyes wide apart and short ears. She had a strong body and
powerful hindquarters. Her thick mane and long tail had
been plaited and her coat brushed to a high sheen. She had
an iron snaffle bit and was caparisoned in a finely stitched
harness decorated with ornamental metal discs.

The chieftain – for this surely was Cunicatus – sat upon
her in the hot midsummer sun with his back straight,
shoulders wide, broad chest forward, head held high and
chin jutting out. He was a muscular man. There were grey
hairs in his beard and in his plaited hair, yet it came to the
boy that here before them was a man in the prime of his
vitality. Quintus had never seen so prideful a man as this.
His bearing upon the big brown mare was like that of an
emperor receiving tribute. An extraordinary performance.

Behind the chieftain came his warriors. They too rode
proudly, packed close together, their smaller horses tightly
reined, jostling against one another. Leather squeaked;

harness jingled. The horses stamped and snorted, breathing heavily under the hot sun. The men all wore helmets and carried spears or javelins. Their tunics and trousers had woven patterns and were brightly coloured: red, blue, yellow. One or two had a scalp, others a skull, hung from a front pommel of their saddles. Provocations.

After these barbarian nobles came infantry, half-naked men. Quintus had heard of the painted people, and here they were, their bodies and faces coloured with swirling circles and intricate patterns, all in blue. Each carried a spear and a shield, scrawled with shapes like those on their bodies. Accounts were given of their ferocious demeanour in battle, but unlike their superiors these men did not seem able to perform the role of fierce combatants or triumphal braggarts, and looked woebegone. They followed their lord and walked between two rows of legionaries, who stood in utter stillness behind their unembellished shields, each in his brown tunic, his helmet and plated armour, betraying no evidence of either complacency or trepidation. A truce had been declared. Quintus did not know whether this chieftain was wise to trust it. 'A Roman is true to his word' was a maxim uttered across the empire, but he knew his master and that this was so only when it suited him.

Above a planked stage his master, Sextus Julius Frontinus, Governor of Britannia, sat upon a large wooden throne the carpenters had made for him the day before.

It was bare, unadorned, of rough timber, but constructed to an elevation sufficient for him to look straight into the eyes of the man approaching him, even sat high as he was upon his handsome mount.

Cunicatus reined in his horse ten yards from the governor. His nobles came to a jostling stop behind him, and beyond them the foot soldiers likewise. The chieftain pricked his horse and walked on, then pulled violently upon the reins, bringing the horse back up on her hindquarters. He let the mare return four hooves to the hard ground then, with his hands on the reins and his legs snug astride the animal's belly, turned her round and around on the spot. The horse trembled and snorted. She seemed to be both struggling against the exercise and revelling in it, her hooves churning the dry earth so that flecks of hard mud spun out in all directions and dust rose around them, a vortex of dust that horse and rider turned within. The specks of mud could be heard striking soldiers' shields, the wooden throne, the governor's armour. Quintus, behind his master's left shoulder, wanted to close his eyes for protection but could not take them off the sight before him. He watched mesmerised. He could feel the power of the animal, and of the man driving her.

Then abruptly they came to a halt, once more facing Frontinus, horse and rider each perspiring freely, breathing heavily, brown dust on their habiliments and stuck to their sweated skin. The chieftain advanced some yards, and stopped and addressed the governor, behind whose right shoulder stood his official interpreter, old Appius. He leaned forward and spoke his translation. Quintus stood close enough to hear him.

'The barbarian says you would surely prefer his horse.'

Quintus reckoned what the chieftain had really said was not that the governor would prefer the horse but that he would benefit more from it. The boy understood the barbarian language better than Appius. Why, even his spoken Latin was superior. But he was a slave. His master would receive his thoughts in private, might ask if things had been missed. Nuances of meaning. He had eavesdropped on many conferences in his master's retinue, and could only be patient.

Frontinus chuckled and said that perhaps he would prefer the horse but that there was no precedent for peace being brokered through the exchange of even so fine an animal as this. Not that he had ever heard of, anyway. He said he knew that the British were horse breeders and dealers and had seen their beasts throughout his travels across the continent, particularly in Gaul, but none better than this one.

The interpreter translated. The chieftain said, 'So be it.' It had to be the way that it was. He would keep the horse then.

The governor said, 'Unless you wish to add it to your gift. We can call it her dowry.'

When he heard the translation, the chieftain's eyes narrowed. He stared at the governor. The governor returned his gaze, a sardonic smile upon his lips.

The boy watched the barbarian king, the most powerful ruler in this part of the country, this land of warring tribes: Cunicatus stared at Frontinus, cold fury fixed in that abject ruler's blue eyes. He did not twitch a muscle. The only life was in those eyes, and it was unwavering hatred.

Abruptly, the chieftain moved, raising his right leg behind him and over the rear pommels of his saddle. He slid off the horse. As he did so he reached across with his right hand and, half-hidden by the horse, stepping back from it, withdrew his sword from its scabbard. Severus and the rest of the bodyguards around the governor shifted forward, ready to protect Frontinus should this warrior approach. He did not. Instead, letting go of the reins of the mare grasped in his left hand, he drew the blade of his sword across the back of her left hind leg, slicing through her hamstring.

Quintus saw in the mare's eyes a look of bewilderment. Her leg buckled, she sank on that knee, then the knee too gave way. Her rider backed away as she toppled over and lay on her left side, her right flank rising and falling in abbreviated breaths.

Cunicatus looked once more at the governor. 'Accept this wedding gift from me,' he said. 'We hear you Romans enjoy the taste of horsemeat.'

While Appius relayed this message in Latin, the chieftain turned and walked towards his jostling throng of mounted troops. The first he reached dismounted and handed the reins to his lord, who took them and led the small horse back in the direction of the ford. A shabby man came lumbering past him, coming up around the warriors and advancing as far as the fallen horse. He seemed to be pursued, hounded, by a stumbling youth.

The beautiful mare lay mute and dignified in her distress.

The scruffy figure was a squat man of indeterminate age, somewhere perhaps between middle and late years. He was mostly bald, with a straggly grey beard and whiskers. Around his shoulders was a long woollen cloak dyed a blueish purple, but a long time ago, and now its blackberry colour was faded, the cloak frayed and torn. The man wore a necklace of teeth, whether animal or human Quintus was not sure. He shuffled slowly, accompanied by the spindly youth, who wore a similarly ragged cloak and was weighed down by various items he carried in a bundle overflowing some kind of tray. Both lacked sandals and wore rags wrapped around their feet.

One of the Druid's eyes was open, the other closed; whether voluntarily, temporarily or for good, Quintus could not tell. The young acolyte separated from his jumble of miscellany something shapeless and passed it to the shaman, who raised it and placed it upon his bald skull. It was a headdress made of feathers from falcons and hawks, from swans or geese. In amongst the muddle of feathers were bones which by their differing size appeared to have come from a variety of animals.

The Druid bent to his apprentice's armful of objects and picked through them, considering one, then another, then the first one again, unable, it seemed, to make up his mind. He had the appearance and the behaviour of a halfwit. Finally, he selected what looked like a clay vessel. He held it by a leather thong upside down, so anything inside would fall out. But nothing did. He took a step or two nearer to the governor sitting impatiently on his throne, and swung the clay cup. It was a bell, which tinkled dully, unimpressively.

The shaman turned away, then stopped. He appeared distracted. Like a man who has just realised he forgot to snuff out the candle when he left his dwelling. He stumbled towards his apprentice, gave back the bell, then grabbed the tray and wrenched it from the grasp of the youth, who did his best to scoop its sundry contents from the air as they dropped to the ground. He was partially successful. The Druid returned to where he had stood, beside the horse, who lay as she had, still, unable to move or unwilling to try, waiting with great dignity to be released from her misery.

8

Then the Druid nodded to the governor, as if in agreement with something Frontinus had said earlier. He lowered his head, gazing at the ground, perhaps considering what it was he agreed with, then raised his head and nodded again at the governor in apparent confirmation. Then he turned his back and faced the Celtic cavalrymen. He lifted the tray. It was circular, a wide band of wood with some animal skin stretched tight across it. Goat, perhaps. Two pebbles hung on strings on opposite sides. It was not a tray.

Holding the drum with his right hand, the Druid flipped his wrist one way, then the other, making the drum swing. He did so with surprising force and rapidity. The two pebbles swung on their strings and struck the goatskin – one on one side, then the other on the converse – with a loud rhythmic resonance. The Druid made a sort of little dance, which was less a dance than employing his body to help the momentum, and thus the speed and noise, of the drumming.

Ahead of him the mounted warriors and their war ponies grew restless. The ponies were packed so tight, and it became apparent that the riders were urging them ever closer to each other, and they resisted. Their nostrils flared and their eyes widened. They whinnied their frustration.

The Druid lowered the drum. The pebbles hung loose. The sudden absence of noise was like a bang, a thump of silence that was itself a signal. The cavalrymen broke out, each away from the centre, like a flower opening all at once and the petals falling away. They rode out, and one after the other turned from the Roman governor and cantered after their chieftain. They rode on either side past the infantrymen, who then turned and trotted after them.

Where the mounted troops had just scrummed in close congregation, there remained one horse, one rider. Seated on the black pony was a young woman, in a pale blue cloak glittering with countless specks of gold. Its collar was the white winter fur of a stoat or ermine. She had red hair, and a gold torc around her neck, and golden bracelets at her wrists. The horse's mane and tail were plaited like her father's mare's and festooned with red, yellow and blue wildflowers.

Quintus could not breathe. His knees were weak, his footing suddenly unsteady. He felt a strong grip on his arm. 'Pull yourself together, slave,' Severus hissed at him.

The tremor passed. Quintus beheld the girl on the horse. Neither she nor her mount, nor any other in the field, seemed to have noticed the ground quake.

Evidently the shaman had given the drum back to his assistant. He now had a skin flask, from which he removed the stopper and drank as he walked over to the young woman. When he reached her it became clear he had not swallowed the liquid but held a mouthful within bulging cheeks. He raised his face and spat the liquid at her. Most landed on her gown. Some on her face. She did not flinch. The Druid shambled past her and followed after the others who had left, his apprentice close behind him.

The girl pricked her horse and walked it slowly towards the governor. She had her father's arrogant bearing and his angry eyes, though hers were green. She looked from one side to the other, her contemptuous gaze falling upon random Roman soldiers and motley staff in turn. For a second her eyes met those of Quintus and lingered for a moment. He felt again his knees soften.

Olwen, daughter of Cunicatus, chief of the Dilovi tribe, ignored her father's lacerated horse and walked hers past it, then stopped the pony a few yards from the governor's throne. Only then did she look up at him.

'Welcome,' Frontinus said. The elderly translator spoke it in her language.

Olwen did not at first respond to the greeting. Then she simply said, 'I am here.'

2

Two soldiers led the girl to a small tent and left her. Inside was a low, slatted wooden couch for a bed, with wool blankets neatly folded upon it. In a corner was a bucket. On a low table were provisions: an amphora of wine, a twisted loaf of bread, a bowl of carrots, a lump of cheese.

Towards nightfall the elderly interpreter came to the tent. He was accompanied by a soldier and stood behind him, a step to one side. Did he think she might bite him? 'The governor will send for you when he is ready,' the interpreter informed her.

'Tell him,' the girl said, 'that when he is ready, I may not be.'

The old man frowned. 'He has important matters on his…' He paused, and tapped his balding skull. 'To discuss, with his generals. He will send for you when he is ready.'

'Tonight?' Olwen asked.

'Tonight,' the old man agreed. 'Or perhaps another night. When he is ready.'

'Unless he enjoys a woman's blood,' she said, 'tell him not tonight.'

The interpreter grinned. A sly, malicious grin. 'Sextus Julius Frontinus had a dream,' he said. 'He dreamed of a woman who pleased him, and he sent envoys over all the earth. Here at last they found you: Olwen, daughter of Cunicatus. And so my master became governor of this hideous island at the edge of the world. All because in a dream he met a woman who might please him. All because of you.'

The girl nodded. 'Is this true?' she asked.

The old man cackled. 'Of course not,' he said. He took a pace back, further behind the soldier. 'Who do you think you are?' He turned and left the tent. The soldier followed him.

Quintus lay down to sleep beneath a blanket on the ground, outside the barrack tent he shared with a dozen other men. He had heard enough of their ribald commentary on the events to which they were proximate.

He dreamed of running. On errands, with messages. Across the tented camp. Which was also, somehow, Ephesus, the distant city of his childhood. Then he dreamed he could not breathe. He was being suffocated. Smothered. He woke to find a hand on his mouth, and struggled. But he saw in

14

the moonlight that it was her. 'Shhh,' she whispered, and lifted her palm from his lips. 'Can you run?'

An odd question. Had she peered into his dream? Quintus did not hesitate. He rose and followed her, slipping past the night watch and out of the camp.

At the ford she expected a guard. There had been a truce, but she was not sure her father had ever observed one he did not like. Perhaps the Romans knew he never attacked at night – just as the Dilovi knew the Romans never did either.

She bade Quintus wait, while she herself walked across. On the far bank she raised her white cloak, which was speckled with flakes of gold that sparkled subtly in the moonlight. She lifted it up, over her legs, above her waist, and on, over her shoulders and her head. Beneath it she wore a short tunic not unlike Quintus's. On her feet were strong sandals, like his. She held the cloak by its neck, lifted her tunic and wiped the white cloth between her legs. When she brought it out, Quintus could see that it was smudged there. Smeared with blood. She dropped it on the ground on the far side of the river and came back across the ford, then turned upstream.

The season was high summer. There had been little rain for weeks and the water level was low, but in the middle of the river the water flowed waist-high and fast. Olwen waded close to the bank. Where the shallowness of water allowed, she ran. Quintus followed close behind, splashing after her. The excitement and terror in his head left no room for any action other than obedience. He was not tired. In time he became calm, and soon saw only the moving form before him and the black water they scurried through.

Occasionally where the river had curved in its tongued passage through soft earth a pool had formed, and this they waded into. The night was warm and they perspired with the exertion, yet the water had come down from the high mountains and was cold, numbing their feet and calves. It was not an unpleasant combination.

Olwen had stopped. Quintus collided with her, and grabbed her shoulders to keep her balance and his own. She turned. 'How could you understand me?' she said. 'When I asked if you could run.'

'I have an ear for languages,' he said.

She stared at him as if waiting for him to say something that made more sense. Then she leaned forward. She reached up, turned his head, pulled aside his tightly curled black hair and studied his ear as well as she could in the partial light. 'It appears to be like any other,' she said. 'Is the other one the same?'

'I believe so. I have not seen them myself.'

'Is it magic that allows you to speak our tongue?'

'I know no magic.'

'There was a woman in our tribe who was spreading skins on her roof and fell from the ladder. She was struck to sleep. When she woke, she spoke a strange language. We thought that was magic. Munatius came and listened. He considered it was probably that of the old forest dwellers, the ones who came before us. Her soul had been rapped back into its earlier form. It was not magic either.'

'It is not my ears but what lies between them, I suppose.'

'Why did you not say so?' Olwen shook her head. 'We have no time to waste on riddles.' She turned back, and they ran on.

The river had made its own floodplain across the wide valley. It meandered through the flatland, in curlicues and lazy convolutions. Olwen took no shortcuts. They splashed across pebbles or gravel beds. There were sandbanks, miniature beaches incongruous on this winding river.

Quintus heard a whooshing beat, and without knowing what it was or where it came from, he ducked. Then he realised the sound was the beating of wings as a pair of ducks flew overhead in the darkness. Olwen had not reacted. Nor did she seem to have noticed his panic. He hurried after her.

The water sparkled. Quintus looked up and saw that as well as the moon, the sky was full of stars. He had grown up on the Asian shore of the Aegean, lived in Rome, travelled across the empire with his master. Yet each night the sun set and the same stars looked down. He stumbled, lowered his gaze and ran on. There were silvery fish in the water. Eels swam amongst the stars.

Olwen stopped once more. Without turning around she reached back and touched Quintus on the arm and pointed across to the far side, a little further upriver. At first he did not know why, but he peered and saw the statue of a heron stood upon the high bank, in lonely vigil. 'Does it approve of us?' Olwen whispered. 'It may ask the spirit of the river to keep our passage secret from those bound to set off in pursuit of us.'

They proceeded carefully, but when they were almost level with the heron it leaned forward and let itself fall onto the air and opened its wings. With wide, elegant flaps it sailed away upriver, low above the water.

Light did not enter the sky. Darkness eased from it. The stars vanished discreetly one by one, snuffed out as by some nightwatchman doing his morning round in the far distance of the firmament.

A tiny bird flew past them at great speed downriver, a streak of blue in the morning. Olwen stopped. 'We should drink,' she said. They waded to where the water was deep, and cupped their hands and swallowed. When they returned to the side she said, 'Out.' Quintus climbed onto the bank. She held out her hand and he took it and pulled her out too, though she clearly did not need him to.

Quintus glanced at her legs and balked. He looked at his own, and made an exclamation of disgust at the black slugs stuck to them. Olwen laughed and said they were only leeches, they would not poison him. She pulled them off him one by one. Where the parasites were attached, she pressed his skin with thumb and forefinger and drew it taut. Then she slid a fingernail under the leech's mouth and separated it, then flicked it away. She told Quintus to let her see if there were any more. 'Hold your arms up,' she said, and when he acquiesced, she lifted his tunic over his head.

Olwen removed four or five leeches. When she was done, she told Quintus to wash the wounds, for he was bleeding from them. He returned to the river while Olwen removed leeches from herself. While she did so she told him how useful these creatures could be. She had once been sent to stand in a river to collect them upon her, and take them to be put to a woman with poisoned blood. 'They sucked the bane from her,' she told him.

They wrung out what water they could from their tunics. When she had washed her own wounds, Olwen moved past Quintus and set off at a run south away from the River Hafren.

3

OLWEN trotted beside the Miwl. Quintus followed. The narrow watercourse had carved a deep tapering gorge for its passage. A damp and gloomy canyon. Trees rose thin and frail for light, their trunks all wrapped around with ivy. Olwen paused to rest.

'When did you form this plan?' Quintus asked her.

'What plan?'

'For us to flee together. You and me.'

She shook her head. 'Until I saw your master I had prepared myself for his dominion over me. I set my life aside, for the good of my tribe. But then I met him and could not bear it.' Olwen paused, lowered her head, then raised it once more. 'I had no plan,' she told Quintus. 'I resolved to leave the Roman camp and make my way home. Then I saw you sleeping in the open, and woke you.'

He said, 'You act as you wish to, in the moment.'

Olwen shrugged. 'I am the daughter of Cunicatus,' she said. 'Chief of the Dilovi.'

Who gave you to his enemy, Quintus thought. But he said nothing.

They crossed the little river over a wooden bridge and climbed through a bwlch or pass. Cow parsley and yellow buttercups grew in profusion by the path. Heading south, they recrossed the Miwl further upstream, where it was narrow and easy to splash through. It had etched an almost circular loop, as if to lasso a wooded knoll with water. The land sloped up from the valley through an oak wood.

'Come,' Olwen said, and veered off the path.

He followed her through scrub and a deep thicket of dogwood into a small glade, and there, hanging from the branches of a thorn tree, were disparate, unusual items to be found in a secluded stretch of woodland. A sword in a coppery scabbard. A goatskin flask. A bow, and a quiver of arrows. A pouch in which was flint, a lump of iron sulphide and tinder. Nettle rope. A woollen blanket.

Quintus said, 'I thought that you had no plan. That you were prepared to be the wife of your father's enemy.'

'This,' she said, opening her arms to take in the items around them. 'This was more like a funeral. A burial of weapons. Farewell to who I was.'

Her iron sword was short, elegant, with a finely wrought handle.

'I had heard of the great iron swords of your people,' Quintus said. 'Such as your father's.'

'I can barely lift my father's sword,' Olwen said. 'How would I wield it in battle? I could not. This one was forged for me.'

Olwen carried her weapons, Quintus the provisions, and thus equipped they walked on.

'Back at the ford,' Quintus said, 'you wiped your blood on your cloak and left it there for them to find.'

'Yes,' Olwen said.

'Why?'

'So they will think you took me by force, and harmed me.'

He looked askance at her. She did not return his gaze, though she surely knew it was upon her. 'I thought so. I suppose I am in even more trouble than I would have been.'

'Even as we speak, a squad of Roman soldiers pursue us. I hope that if they think you took me, they will under-estimate us.'

Quintus shook his head. 'How can you say such a thing?'

'Forgive me,' Olwen replied. 'But you are an interpreter. You are clearly not a warrior.'

———

They climbed through a deep zawn or crevice with steep wooded sides. The path beside the trickle of water at the bottom of the dingle was overgrown with brambles here and there, and they had constantly to lift their legs and tread them down. Their shins and calves were scratched and cut. They emerged in the open and had taken a few steps when Olwen slowed her pace and said, 'We are being watched.'

Quintus stopped and began to crouch.

Olwen touched his arm. 'Look you,' she said, gesturing off to one side.

A beast, a cat of some kind, sat on a rock higher up the slope, where it had been sunning itself until being disturbed by these noisy bipeds. Its fur was brown, almost red, with darker spots across its body. It had a beard of lightly coloured fur sprouting from its jaw, and the same within its large upright ears. Each ear had a black tuft of hair growing from it. It sat on its back paws and rump, utterly still, observing them with placid brown eyes. There emanated from it neither fear nor aggression. More a dispassionate study.

'A lynx,' Olwen whispered.

Then, as if receiving an abrupt request to be elsewhere, the lynx shifted. It did not move like an animal composed of a skeleton with joints to be articulated, bones to be levered. The cat's flesh flowed into motion, and then all its paws were on the ground and it padded away and vanished into the shadows of juniper trees. Quintus turned to Olwen and saw that she had bowed her head towards the departing creature and was muttering what sounded like a prayer.

Olwen barely registered the rain clouds in the sky, yet all of a sudden sweeping ribbons of soft warm water brushed over them. The rainwater swayed to and fro, as if some giant peasant strolled across the heath dipping his maul into his sack, casting not seed but raindrops, this way and that. Then he moved on. The light rain had barely impinged upon their clothing and done little more than stain the landscape, toning all its colours slightly darker.

A pair of black birds, with black beaks, flew high overhead. They came lower, kronking loudly as if in greeting. For a while they accompanied the two youths, performing acrobatics in the air, playing with each other, perhaps putting on a display for the human audience, or possibly mocking their earthbound status.

Olwen told Quintus that of all the birds she knew, ravens seemed to be the ones who enjoyed themselves the most.

Approaching the Ceri ridge, climbing through pasture grass littered with dandelions, buttercups, white clover, Olwen stopped abruptly. Assuming she had seen something, Quintus drew level with her and looked around. He turned to her. Her mouth was closed and she breathed through her nose, deeply. She closed her eyes: with long inhalations, she processed the air in her nostrils. Then he smelled it too. Meat cooking.

They walked towards the aroma. A pale wisp of smoke rose in the blue sky, and soon they found three youths roasting a spit of mutton. Two boys, one girl. Beyond them was a flock of thirty or forty sheep, grazing on the upland grass. The first boy to see them approach jumped up, grabbing his crook. The second boy turned and saw them, and whistled. The girl stood.

Olwen neither paused nor waved to the shepherds but carried on walking towards them at the same steady pace. Quintus followed her lead. The dog had not been far away and came promptly. He was a muscly creature. The hackles on his back rose and he growled at the newcomers, barring their way.

Now Olwen stopped. 'Call your dog off,' she said.

None of them moved. The dog snarled, baring his teeth.

'I have no wish to have to silence it myself,' Olwen said.

The boy who had whistled for the guard dog did not respond, but the girl said, 'Do it,' and he stirred from his sullen inertia and walked towards the dog, talking to it, ordering it to cease its prickly welcome. He grasped its leather collar and said, 'Come,' and yanked it off to one side.

Olwen and Quintus walked on to the fire. The boy there stood gaping.

'Do you need your stick to turn the meat?' Olwen asked him.

The boy looked down at the staff in his hand. He appeared surprised to find it there, and dropped it.

Olwen laid down her bow, unbuckled her scabbard and sat cross-legged on the ground. Quintus remained standing, waiting until these two sat as well and the other boy had tied up his guard dog and returned. Olwen patted the turf beside her, glancing up at him. Warily, he joined her.

The meat cooked in the flames of the small fire on wooden skewers resting in V-shaped notches of sticks pushed into the earth. Fat from the meat dripped onto the flames, making them sizzle. Saliva manifested itself in Quintus's mouth.

'Please,' the girl said. 'Help yourself.'

'We do not wish to take your food,' Olwen told her.

'We have more,' the boy assured her. 'We have plenty.'

They took a skewer each and nibbled the hot meat, then as it cooled chewed delicious mouthfuls. The shepherds themselves did not eat but sat watching their transient guests, joined now by the other boy. Quintus could see the dog some yards away, roped to a tree, already snoozing. The meat was crackly on its outside, tender within. He sucked all he could from the bones.

Between the girl and the boy in charge of the dog was a pile of nettles. The boy put on a pair of leather gloves and stripped the leaves. The girl slit the denuded stalks with a small knife and extracted their interior matter. She passed the outer bark to the first boy, who plaited the strips into an ever-enlarging ball of string. This boy addressed Olwen. 'Is he a Roman?'

As if she was of like mind, about to utter that selfsame question, the girl said, 'Because he wears a Roman tunic, and sandals, but his skin is so dark.'

The boy frowned. 'His hair is so curly.'

The second boy said, 'They all have dark skin.'

'Not as dark as his,' the girl said. 'Nor so handsome.'

They spoke of Quintus as if he were a mute who could not hear them. Or more likely they assumed he could not understand what they said.

'Have you seen Romans?' Olwen asked them.

The girl nodded. 'They buy our sheep.'

'And drink our barley beer,' the second boy said, and the others laughed.

'Look at you,' Olwen said. 'Look at us. We have sold our animals and we have sold ourselves, betrayed by our parents' generation. Our grandparents would never have given away their birthright so cheaply. We have been humiliated. We have lost our freedom. We should be ashamed.' She put her palm to the turf and, leaning into it, raised herself

28

cross-legged off the ground and stood. 'Thank you for the meat. But yours are no longer free people. You might as well be captives. Slaves. Perhaps one day your grandchildren will rise up and reclaim your dignity. If you still have the spunk to make children and the wombs to carry them.'

She lifted her weapons, and turned and set forth. Quintus climbed to his feet, gathering the bags. He thanked the young shepherds and followed her.

When he caught up, he said, 'How did you know they would not attack us? They were younger than us, but there were three of them and they had a ferocious dog.'

Olwen kept walking but turned to him with a frown. 'Shepherds?' she asked. 'A shepherd would never attack a warrior. Farmers have no training. They are not permitted. It would be suicide.' She was stupefied by Quintus's ignorance. 'And if a warrior was known to have attacked a farmer? Their reputation would be ruined beyond repair.' She could hardly believe what he did not know. 'They would do well to dig their own unmarked grave, in a lonely place, and lie in it, and pull the soil in handfuls upon themselves, and perish there, hoping the news of their dishonour will be buried with them.'

'Does the dog understand these subtleties?'

'They are Ordovice. The whole tribe are cowards. Even their guard dogs. If our pursuers question them, all they know will spill from their mouths.'

'Perhaps the young have more mettle than their elders?'

'Cowardice is in their blood. They cannot help it. Still, I am grateful to them, to have a full belly.'

As they spoke, Quintus realised that the tempo of their stride was accelerating. They walked more briskly. Like a bow being drawn back. Then Olwen broke into a trot.

They crossed the ridgeway. Olwen turned and stood and surveyed the undulant wooded landscape through which they'd climbed.

'Do you see anything?' Quintus asked.

Olwen gazed a while longer. 'No,' she said. 'But they are there.'

All around them were small twisted and gnarled trees that had withstood the wild winds of many winters. They passed between two mounds that Olwen said were tumuli or tombs, for the cremated remains of farmers hereabouts. Generations of a family in each tomb. Quintus said they didn't look like they'd been used for centuries. Olwen shrugged. 'A family dies out,' she said. 'The tomb is abandoned.'

The landscape rolled endlessly, like kneaded dough suddenly hardened. They padded up, and clambered down, through the long, hot day. On trails made by driven beasts, on footpaths, on animal tracks.

'Are you sure of the right direction?' Quintus asked.

'I know every hill,' she told him. 'Every stream. I have known them all my life.'

He asked her how old she was. She told him she was nineteen.

'I am the same,' he told her.

They crossed the River Teme and climbed through a wood. Its oak trees were slim, elegant and curving. Or gently twisting, as if they had in their own slow conversance with time been dancing upwards. These trees gave to the hillside a dappled shade. The oak leaves and grass and bracken were closely aligned tints of green.

They followed a brook upstream, south of the river, where it fed into the larger watercourse. After a short distance Olwen said, 'We shall find a place to camp.'

She set down her weapons at the base of an old oak and leaned her forehead against its knuckly trunk. Quintus saw that her lips were moving. Was she whispering to the tree? He searched in the warm dusk for dry grass for tinder, and twigs for kindling, and broken branches. A flock of pigeons took off, wings beating with a sound like clapping hands, as if applauding their own flight.

Night fell. Darkness enveloped them in its safe embrace. They lit the fire. Olwen sharpened the blade of her sword with a small lump of abrasive sandstone.

Quintus asked her what she had said to the oak tree. She told him that every living thing had its own spirit, and each spirit had its own value and its own worth, and might help them if it wished to.

'You asked the oak tree to help us?'

Olwen nodded. 'I prayed to the spirit of the oak that it might keep us safe through this night to come.'

It had been many hours since they ate the shepherds' meat. Amongst the possessions Olwen had stashed in the thorn scrub, she had not thought to request food beyond a single loaf of bread, itself like the rest more emblem than actual provision. Now it was all they had, and they broke it into hard chunks, then into smaller segments. These they held on their tongues until their saliva had softened the dry, stale bread a little, before chewing it slowly and drinking water from the goatskin flask.

Quintus was so tired he fell asleep still chewing. When he jerked awake, he was surprised to find soggy bread in his mouth. Olwen lay on the ground. He lay down beside her.

In the middle of the night Olwen awoke. She listened to sounds that came from the darkness. Utterances of animals. Their movement rustling. Trees creaking. Where were the stars? She rose and walked out of the wood. Pale clouds sailed gently across the sky like puffs of breath. Of smoke exhaled by some giant over the horizon. She stood and watched a white owl quarter the upland meadow, hunting for voles.

Olwen asked herself why she had taken flight. And why had she invited this Roman slave to join her? He looked unlike anyone she had ever seen. He was striking, beautiful. Was that all the reason she had needed?

She returned to the oak tree and lay down. She listened to Quintus's breathing but could barely hear it. 'Are you awake?' she whispered.

'No,' he replied.

'You are,' she said.

'I am,' he conceded. 'Now.'

Quintus felt sensation on his skin, and realised that Olwen was tentatively stroking his arm. His chest. He turned to face her, though he could not see her, and stroked her skin too.

He embraced her, and she embraced him. They held one another tight and kissed and caressed in the dark. Quintus explored Olwen's body blindly, as she did his, and in doing so they discovered their own. When they were ready, she took him into her, and they possessed each other.

Afterwards, Quintus lay on his back and Olwen lay against him. She said she had wondered what it would feel like. He said he had wondered the same thing, and now he knew and was glad of it. He was happy. He asked if it had given her pleasure. Had she enjoyed it? She said she had, very much. He said he was even happier about that. And then they had said enough as they lay together, and Olwen soon fell asleep.

Their fire dwindled. Quintus could not revive it without disturbing Olwen. The moon waned. He listened. He heard sounds of movement. Of animal grunts, cries, calls. He had heard them before, but always from inside the camp. Now he was outside, amongst them, and he could not help picturing what made those noises. He saw grotesque creatures. Horrible beasts. Until he slipped back into sleep and they appeared no more.

4

THEY rose early in the morning and set forth, hungry. A mist covered the land. They climbed out of lowland woods, into high meadows. Quintus looked up and saw through the mist the white disc of the moon. He watched it a while, then nudged Olwen and gestured towards it and said, 'Behold, the moon rising.'

On they walked. The day was already warming. He became aware of her trembling beside him. He asked whether she was cold.

Olwen did not reply but kept her mouth closed tight and shook her head, and walked on briskly. He watched her but she would not look at him. She seemed to be biting the insides of her cheeks. Her lips quivered.

Quintus said, 'So tell me, what is so funny? I can see you are trying not to laugh at me.'

Olwen turned to him, still tight-lipped. But she was unable to suppress the smile upon her face. She gestured to the sky, grinning. The mist had thinned a little more and Quintus was able to discern the moon more clearly. He saw that it was not the moon but the sun, a silver burning globe.

'Anyone might have made the same mistake,' he said. 'This infernal fog.'

'I saw the moon arising in the morning,' Olwen said, giggling.

Quintus lunged at her, furious, or pretending to be. She bent and turned and ran away. He ran after her, and thus did they begin to run on that the second day.

The sun rose and burned off the mist until all that remained were ribbons of white, each tracing a river or stream below them. They stood on a shelf of rock and looked back, north across a range of mountains, past what Olwen said were the Berwyns to the Aran range and Yr Wyddfa beyond. Quintus observed that each further summit on this clear morning was a paler green than the one before, and more enticing. Olwen told him that was nonsense, they were not enticing, he should never go there. That wild people lived in the caverns and canyons of those mountains. She said they stole children and ate human flesh. That they dragged their frail elderly to certain crags and left them there for the red kites. 'While the poor old folk still breathe!' she emphasised.

As they trotted on, south-west, into the heat of the day, she enumerated further crimes committed routinely by those savages of the north. Then they dropped down into meadowland, where buttercups and campion and wild-flowers whose names Olwen did not know grew amongst the tall summer grasses. Bees and wasps, beetles and flies droned between the flowers. Orange butterflies fluttered around their heads. The sound of grasshoppers chirping grew louder and the smell of high summer, musky and sweet, ever stronger.

Olwen wore a gold torc around her neck. It had a flattened inner surface which sat snug against her skin, an outer decoration of spherical knobs. Quintus had seen her take it off to wash. It was constructed from two parts, three-quarters of a circle joined to a quarter by a dowel at one point and a pinned hinge at the other. He had noticed torcs before. Many were highly ornamented. This was such a simple design.

'Your torc is very beautiful,' Quintus said.

Olwen nodded. She looked around. 'Let's rest a moment,' she said, and lay down on some grass beside a pond. She drank from their flask and passed it to Quintus. When he had finished, he replaced the stopper.

Olwen plucked a daisy, snapping the green neck of its stem where it emerged from its collar of leaves, then did the same with another. With her thumbnail she cut a slit near the end of the stem, then slid the stem of the second daisy through the slit as far as its flowered head. She cut a slit in this second daisy as she had the first, then tugged a third daisy from the ground and threaded it through likewise.

Red damselflies and dragonflies flew above the still water of the pond.

When Olwen had made a chain composed of twenty or thirty of these organic links she pushed the head of the first daisy through a new slit in the stem of the last, and raised what was now a necklace. She hung it in front of Quintus. He bowed his head towards her. Olwen looped the daisy chain over his head. It settled on his shoulders. 'There,' she said. 'A torc for you.'

Quintus kissed her. 'Thank you, princess,' he said.

'My consort,' she whispered, and kissed him too.

Olwen rose to her feet. They had lingered too long. She reached out her hand. He took it, and she pulled him up.

They climbed a broad hill, and as they came to the heights the forest opened up and they walked over the bare tonsured summit of the hill. There were two more burial mounds here, and Olwen climbed on one to see if there were sight of their pursuers.

'There,' she said, and pointed.

Quintus joined her and peered in the direction she had indicated. From where they had come, and all around, looked like solid forest. A rolling ocean in shades of green. The tops of the tallest tree canopies rustling and swaying in the fresh breeze.

'In a clearing,' Olwen said. 'I saw figures, marching.'

'How many?'

She shook her head. 'I don't know.'

They descended from the mound and carried on. After a while Quintus felt Olwen's hand grip his arm.

'Look you.' She gazed upwards. Quintus peered and saw a bird of prey approaching. He could not tell its size until it came closer and flew directly overhead. It was large, with a wide wingspan and a long tail, a light grey body and grey-blue-coloured head, and flew with a quivering flight. The tips of its wings were black. It was very beautiful.

They turned to watch it, and as if for their observance the bird wheeled in the sky and came back around.

'What does it have in its talons?' Quintus asked. 'It's carrying something.'

'Something it has killed,' Olwen said. 'Listen.'

They heard a faint whistling. Olwen said the hen harrier was calling for his mate. And thus invited, a female rose from her nest in the heather. She was brown and white. They flew in circles and figures of eight close together, in and out of each other's shadows, careful to keep their wings from colliding.

'What are they doing?' Quintus asked. Then he saw the male flip the carcass of his prey in the air, and to his amazement the female caught it in her talons and returned abruptly to her nest.

The male harrier disappeared in the direction whence he had first come. Quintus gazed at the emptying sky. He heard Olwen chuckle beside him.

'If you don't close your mouth,' she said, 'you'll catch a horsefly, and then you'll be sorry.'

Quintus blinked. 'Did that really happen?' he asked. 'Did we really see that?'

They trotted on, down into woodland then up out again across Bare Hill, another scalped summit, covered in hummocks of grass and gorse. Olwen knelt and dipped her hands in amongst plants that grew there. She extracted something and put it in her mouth. 'Behold,' she said.

Quintus knelt beside Olwen and watched her pluck small purple berries. He picked some and ate them. They were tart, but tasty. They ate greedily, then set off again on a path whose long descent down the side of Hill Ground took leisurely deviations around its uneven flanks. The trees thinned out and they crossed the Leithon stream over a narrow wooden bridge.

They climbed again above the treeline, where here and there dotted on the hillside odd trees grew like lonely sentinels sent out to survey the harsh landscape above. Then they descended through sparse bracken and a ribbon of pine back into dense woodland. Out in the open Quintus was terrified of being seen and craved the hidden wood; amongst the trees he panicked at each sound of unseen origin.

Olwen climbed down into the winding Bachell Brook and they splashed through it as they did most waterways, before climbing out some way from where they'd entered. They followed it along a path on its western side.

They could have walked almost as briskly as this loping run, but perhaps it took less energy to trot slowly along than to march as Roman soldiers did. The sun flickered through the canopy. Insects buzzed in the warm late afternoon. Quintus ambled behind Olwen, his mind emptying of thoughts, then of awareness of the vista around him and the landscape into which they advanced. He was not conscious of his eyes closing, but what he saw changed from the vague, blurry shape of Olwen's footsteps ahead of him to being in a dream of a meal in his master's tent. He served wine to the governor and to Severus, commander of his personal bodyguard. Olwen's father was there too. They were discussing or arguing about something, but in

41

whispers, and he could not quite decipher them. He moved surreptitiously around the table to hear what was said, but where he moved the speaker became silent and someone on the other side of the tent was whispering.

He was woken by a touch. He opened his eyes, expecting the caress to be that of Olwen, only to find that although he was still trotting slowly, she was no longer in front of him. Instead, he was in the midst of a small, tight throng of children. They shuffled and capered and skipped along. It was dusk. He could have sworn he and Olwen had been in a wood, but he was now on a narrow path through scrub. He looked around, over the children's heads, and could see no sign of Olwen. Had he veered away from her in his sleep?

The children paid Quintus no heed. They ignored him ostentatiously. Yet he was imprisoned amongst them. He tried to stop, to go in search of Olwen, but they propelled him along, and when he slowed he felt their small bodies press insistently against him and he was unable to resist.

They came out of the scrub into a meadow. Quintus heard noises. Sounds. One was drums. Another was the bleating of sheep. Then he saw them up ahead in the fading light. A procession, not of sheep but of men and women with ram's horns attached to girdles or suchlike contraptions worn upon their heads, and all were shuffling forward with their heads bowed and arms floppy by their sides, and all were bleating their ovine mimicry.

Before and aft of the company, with big drums on straps yoked over their shoulders, were several young, bare-chested men, who pummelled the taut, dark skins of their drums with knobbly sticks. The drummers beat a simple rhythm – Dum. Dum. Dum-dum-dum – walloping repetitively as they advanced.

In the middle of the procession, six women carried a wooden bier or dais on their shoulders. On this platform an old man knelt on all fours. His nakedness was covered in a sheepskin coat, though his slack belly and meagre genitals swayed bare beneath him. The old man also had ram's horns attached to his head. He did not bleat like those below and around him but gazed ahead with an idiotic vacancy.

The children met the procession and joined it. Either they forced their way in or the shepherds allowed it, but they were soon just behind the women carrying the old man on his parodic throne. All were dressed in tatters and rags, whether their normal penurious attire or an exaggeration of their poverty Quintus did not know. The sound of the human flock's plaintive lament hurt his ears.

Quintus heard a child yell, 'Look! Here is the one. We have found him.' But no one looked his way. At least, he did not catch anyone taking notice of him. They stared, but at things that were not there. Yet he felt himself observed.

The queer cortège crossed the meadow. The sun set behind western hills and the meadowland was cast in a strange light reminiscent of oil lamplight, except that there was no direct source of illumination. Everything – the meadow grass, the sheepskin cloak of the old man, the faces of those around him – was cast in this orange-yellow hue.

Quintus looked ahead. Standing in the shallow water of a creek towards which they headed he saw an oddly attired woman of middle age. She wore a long coat of feathers, taken from all manner of birds, many different sizes, colours, thicknesses, sewn together randomly. Her hair was white and black, and wild like the twigs of an abandoned apple tree. As they approached, she raised and put on her head a mask fashioned from the head of a bear, and he understood that she was ordained of the same mould as the Druid attached to Cunicatus. She climbed out and began to dance in little circles on the riverbank. Quintus could not quite tell whether she danced in time to the rhythm of the drummers. She may have been doing so in her own way, though it did not seem right to him.

When they reached the creek, some members of the cavalcade broke off to light lanterns at the end of sharpened stakes they pressed into the soft turf. Others waded across to do likewise on the other side. The water was wider and deeper here, a pond. The shaman now enlarged the circumference of her radial dance, and the procession fell in behind her. The drummers upped the tempo of their beat – DUM dum-dum-dum, DUM dum-dum-dum, DUM DUM DUM.

Those around Quintus were not exactly dancing, at least not as he had ever understood it or done so himself, but were stamping their feet on the ground in time to the beat of the drums. It occurred to him that he had now begun doing so too. The children cavorted, improvising little jigs and twirls, but the adults trudged with solemn concentration and intent. Gradually, one by one, with the giddiness and exertion, they stopped bleating. The grass was rubbed out, and the topsoil crumbled into granules that rose into the air as dust around them and was illuminated by the flaming lanterns. And the drummers kept drumming, and the Druid kept leading the sheep people round and round, all mesmerised.

Quintus must have closed his eyes again, though he did not fall asleep this time and was not dreaming but settled into the rhythm of the circumambulation. Then it changed and he opened his eyes to see that the Druid had stepped back down into the stream. The women carrying the wooden platform set it on the ground, then lifted it up again to bear it at waist height into the water. There they lowered it to float. The drummers ceased their pummelling, breathing hard, lungs heaving. Their bare skin glistened in the lamplight. The devotees crowded on the riverbank, stunned expressions on their faces.

The shaman nodded to a young man who was dressed in similarly eccentric costume, not of feathers but of grass, corn, stems of flowers. He held a bell in front of him and rang it. The Druid reached through an opening in her cloak and pulled out a knife. The women who had borne the platform along grasped hold of the kneeling man, with hands on his shoulders, back and limbs, though it seemed there was little need, for he retained the expression of a simpleton who no longer had any notion of what was happening to him.

The Druid stepped forward in the water and without ceremony cut the old man's throat as she might a lamb's. The women gently lowered him to the bier and he lay curled up like a baby as the life bled out of him. Now the shaman called loudly, fiercely, demanding of their god a good harvest this year, and for their sheep, cattle and goats to keep their flesh through the winter ahead and multiply come spring. It was a brief prayer or exhortation. Then she nodded to the women and they let go of the wooden dais and watched it float downstream.

Quintus and all those on the bank observed the raft snag on an overhanging branch. The current obliged it to perform half a turn about the branch until it slipped free, and continued, and floated out of the orbit of the firelight and disappeared into the darkness beyond.

A man with ram's horns called down to the shaman, 'Look you. We have the one you have told us of. He is here.' He gestured to Quintus, on whom all now gazed openly.

The Druid turned her bear's head towards him. A figure wearing an outfit of feathers with an ursine head, she was not wholly human. She climbed out of the stream and the congregants made way for her to walk unsteadily towards him. The bloodied dagger was still in her hand.

He had heard of the Celtic custom of blood sacrifice. Had this pond been dug out for sacrificial purposes? Frontinus had told him it was his intent to be the Roman governor who would rid the wretched island of this barbaric custom. Now Quintus had seen it. He had been scared witless for two days, with those after him capable of brutality he knew too well. Now he was amongst people he did not know at all, and he was shaking.

'Here is the black lamb who is come to save us,' someone yelled.

The Druid came up close. He saw in the bear's eye sockets her own eyes, appraising him. Her eyes were paler than the moon, white, translucent. He couldn't believe she could see him, but he felt she could see through him, or into him. She leaned in and sniffed him as if with the snout of the bear. He could smell her too, rank, acrid, which was surely the stink of the beast, but perhaps shamans preferred to be unwashed.

She reached up with her free hand and touched his face. His nose. His lips.

'It is he whose coming you have foretold,' a woman said.

The Druid took a step back and shook her bear's head. 'He is not the one,' she said quietly. Quintus heard her. He doubted whether more than one or two others could. But the boy who had rung the bell had come up unseen behind her, and he now repeated, in a thin, half-broken but much louder voice, 'He is not the one.'

A boy close to Quintus called out, 'He has wet himself.'

'He is an imposter,' the Druid said, and her assistant repeated it for all to hear. At once a man here, a woman there resumed their ovine bleating. Others took up the quavering complaint. But it was different now, a cry not of pathos but belligerence. Aggression. The six women who had carried the old man took it upon themselves to come forward and grab hold of Quintus and lift him up by his limbs and head and torso. If they expected him to struggle they were wrong, and they found his body a limp weight to convey into the stream.

The people on the bank ceased their horrible noise and watched, enthralled, as the women carried Quintus into the stream as if his body were already lifeless. He'd feared dying for what Olwen had done, and now he was about to die for not being someone he'd never claimed to be.

There came a yell from the darkness. The women holding his legs let go, and Quintus stood unsteadily in the stream. Olwen emerged into the light from the lanterns, walking downstream through the shallow water. She drew the sword as she approached and the women let go of Quintus and scattered, splashing.

Olwen said to the Druid merely, 'He is mine,' and brushed past Quintus. 'Come,' she said. She climbed out of Clywedog Brook to the bank where the men and women with their ram's horns and the drummers and the children stood gaping. They parted to let her through. Quintus stumbled after her, autonomous control of his limbs clumsily returning to him. He glanced back. The Druid stood in the stream, the bear's head staring after him, the knife still by her side.

They crossed the brook further upstream and climbed up through the forest on the sloping hillside. They made a fire and sat before it. Olwen honed her sword. She looked across at Quintus and asked if he was cold. He lifted his shoulders as if his neck needed warmth. His teeth were chattering.

'Why do you shiver?' Olwen asked.

Quintus shook his head. 'They thought I was their saviour.'

Olwen laughed. 'Peasants always have a saviour who is about to arrive.'

'They told the Druid I was the one she herself had augured, yet then she accused me of fakery.'

'What else would you expect?' Olwen asked. 'What use would a prophet be once the saviour she's predicted actually arrives? She would be rendered superfluous. No wonder she denounced you.'

'It's a good thing there were no warriors there.'

'It is,' Olwen agreed.

'And I'm grateful for the farmers' taboo against fighting.'

Olwen was thoughtful. 'I'm not sure it holds when they're in a trance.'

Moths flew around their heads. Olwen saw them and rose, and vanished from the firelight into the darkness of the wood behind them. Soon she came back, and they sucked the nectar from honeysuckle stems she had collected. She said the smell of honeysuckle was stronger at night.

'I didn't smell it,' Quintus said.

'Neither did I,' Olwen admitted. 'But I saw the moths who could.'

She wrapped one of their blankets around Quintus, and sat beside him and hugged him close to share her body heat. He asked her what the strange sounds were above them. She told him they were made by young owls, wheezing in the trees.

———

The honeysuckle nectar was hardly food. Olwen's stomach rumbled. They made love and their hunger meant their kisses were avid, greedy. They slept deeply, and woke in the dark. There were gleams of green light in the undergrowth around them. Glow-worms. Quintus fed the fire with fresh wood, in the cool depths of night.

'Do you want to hear a story?' Olwen whispered.

'A story? About what?'

'About my family,' she said. 'The royal house of my tribe.'

'I would,' he replied.

'Then I will tell you, my love.' Olwen spoke softly into his ear. 'Long ago there lived in these hills a fine couple, Tegid Voel and his wife, Caridwen. Caridwen gave birth to a girl, who became the fairest maiden in the world. Then she had a son, but this poor boy was hideously ugly. Now Caridwen consulted her Druid, and was told how to make a magical potion that might grant the gift of wisdom and poetic inspiration to the boy, in compensation for his ugliness. Caridwen gathered the ingredients.'

'What kind of ingredients?' Quintus asked.

'Certain herbs,' Olwen told him. 'She was to pick them at particular times advised by the ancient astronomers. These were put in a cauldron, along with water collected in moonlight from the River Towy. The mixture had to be boiled for a year and a day, until it had reduced to just three drops of liquid. So Caridwen set Morda, an old man,

51

to kindle the fire beneath the cauldron, and Gwion Bach, a young boy, to stir the concoction.

'Every day Gwion's curiosity about the potion he stirred grew stronger. He was not the brightest child in those valleys. Perhaps it would make him more intelligent? Day after day he resisted temptation. But after one year, he leaned into the cauldron and put his thumb into the potion, and lo, those last three drops stuck to his thumb. Being so hot, they burned him. He instinctively put his thumb in his mouth, and in that moment gained the wisdom Caridwen had intended for her son. He foresaw all that was to come, including Caridwen's anger and his own death. Gwion fled.

'The next morning, one year and one day from its beginning, Caridwen came in and saw the cauldron was empty. She seized a billet of wood and struck old Morda about the head. He said, "Wrongfully have you disfigured me, for I am innocent. Your loss was not my fault."

'"You speak the truth," said Caridwen, and she went forth after Gwion, running. Soon he saw her after him, and with the powers of the potion he turned himself into a hare. But Caridwen changed herself into a greyhound and ran him down. He leapt into a river and became a fish. But she transformed herself into an otter and chased him under the water. He jumped from the water and became a bird. But she became a hawk and harried him across the sky. On the point of capture, Gwion spied a heap of winnowed wheat on the floor of a barn, and dropped down and turned into a single grain of wheat.

'But Caridwen became a high-crested black hen. She scratched amongst the grains and found him and swallowed him. And that was the end of Gwion.'

'A great story,' Quintus said. 'But a sad end, I think.'

'Wait,' Olwen told him. 'Time passed, and Caridwen realised she was pregnant. She knew that somehow this was Gwion's doing, and resolved to kill the child when it was born.

'But she gave birth to a son so beautiful that she could not do it. She carried him to the ocean instead, and set him in a coracle, and let the tides take him. The coracle was swept out to sea, then back to shore on a lonely beach. It was found by a beachcomber, who took the baby in and raised him as his own. That child became Taliesin, my great-great-great-great-grandfather, who grew up to be the first of the famous bards of my country. And that, Quintus, my love, was his first story.'

Quintus embraced Olwen. 'Thank you,' he said, 'for your first story.'

'Now tell me one,' she replied.

Quintus thought for a while. At length he said, 'I cannot. We did not have such stories.'

'Tell me about your family. Your grandparents, for example.'

'I never knew them.'

'Your parents.'

Again, Quintus considered the matter. Then he said, 'My father came to the city from the east, from Armenia Minor, I think. He came alone, I don't know how or why. He rarely spoke about the past. Ephesus was a city second only to Rome. It had its own amphitheatre, its public square, a town hall. There were bathhouses and public latrines. It received water from reservoirs outside the city, along aqueducts. It had a large man-made harbour. Ships came from the west, caravans from the eastern provinces along the Royal Road.

'My father was ten years old. He went to the market and pilfered wooden boxes that the fruit and vegetable traders tossed into piles behind their stalls. He broke these up into bundles for kindling, which he sold door to door. Depending on the size of the house, he raised or lowered the price. He employed younger children. As he became familiar to house owners or their slaves he asked if there were other things they would like him to deliver. And so by degrees he became a merchant.

'I spent my childhood trotting through the narrow streets. Running errands, carrying messages around the city, the harbour. To ships. I'd run to and fro with bids and counterbids.'

'You carried scrolls? Tablets?'

Quintus chuckled. 'My father wrote nothing down until a deal had been agreed. Then it went into his ledger. I had to memorise each message.'

'You never forgot?'

'No doubt I did.' Olwen could barely see Quintus's face in the dim firelight, but she heard the smile in his voice. 'In a corner of his office, behind cabinets, was a space for me to sleep. Everyone knew my father. He could never remember their names, so he greeted people with a caressing endearment. "Hello, dear friend", or "Precious jewel", or "Exalted one". My sister and I would try to guess which salutation he was going to use on whoever was approaching.'

'He sounds amusing.'

'He could be. I suspect he saw all relationships as transactions: what can I offer you and you offer me? He loved to haggle. Every deal was an endless negotiation until it was finalised. If he agreed to accept two jars of olive oil for an amphora of wine, he'd either forget or ignore the agreement and demand three jars. Until he'd spat on his palm and shaken hands. He was incorrigible, my father, he infuriated people, but they indulged him because he had no ill will. He wasn't trying to hurt people, he invited them to play the game of barter, and most people found they enjoyed it. Even his relationships with his children were the same. "Tell us a story, Daddy." "If you promise to go to sleep in ten minutes." "Two stories, please, Daddy, please." "Two stories. Eight minutes.'"

'Was he handsome, Quintus? But of course he must have been.'

'I think so. He was attractive. He picked the shells off cardamoms and chewed them all day. Other men stank of what they put in their pipes. His breath smelled so enticing. He wasn't very tall, but he was fleshy. Many of his deals were made over long lunches. I also ran with dishes from the harbour restaurants to his warehouse, where he had a room for hosting clients. At home he liked to wrestle with my sister and me: "I'll take you both on!" We always nearly won, but in the end we never did. And we finished laughing so much none of us could fight any more. Our mother's disapproval made it even funnier.'

After a while Olwen realised Quintus had said all he wished to. She kissed him and whispered, 'Goodnight, my love,' and so they slept.

5

I n the morning they rose and climbed hard, further away from the valley where the sacrifice had taken place. When they reached open ground they paused to rest, lungs heaving. They looked back and could see no sign of habitation in the forest far below except for smoke rising here and there in perfect threads, as if gravity had turned upside down.

They walked through rolling hill country. Sparse woodland alternated with open moor, birch carr and alder with valley mire. The birds they saw were shabby, moulting, losing their feathers. Dense forest gave way to grazing pasture, where sheep knelt solemnly to the late summer grass, bleating intermittently as if in complaint at the feeble nourishment. When they crossed what Olwen called Wide Pass they could hear the ringing of axes in the distance. In a holly tree small birds roosted, invisible but chattering, like soldiers entered into a new barracks bickering about which bunk was whose.

———

They walked on pathways between farmsteads, or tracks on which shepherds had driven their sheep or traders their goods, or pilgrims trekked to holy places. Some were roads of earth trodden to a hard surface, others barely discernible trails across rocky slopes, still others hollow ways, sunken lanes.

In a beech wood, Olwen took Quintus by the arm. He looked along her line of sight and caught a brief glimpse of a hawklike bird weaving between the trees, then it was gone. She said it was a sparrowhawk, the smallest bird of prey she knew of. Its wings were short, as he might have noticed, though its tail was long, and it could veer between trees at great velocity, as he must have seen.

A little further on they passed a tree stump on whose surface and around whose base were white and grey feathers. Olwen paused to study them. 'Her plucking post,' she said. 'Where she pulls the feathers from her victims before eating the flesh or taking it to her nest.'

Quintus asked her how she knew it was a female. She told him that a female sparrowhawk is larger than a male.

'And these feathers are those of a dove. And a pigeon. A male sparrowhawk would likely be unable to bring down such heavy birds. He goes for lighter ones, like tits or thrushes.'

They walked on through a copse of elders and crab apple. Quintus plucked one and bit into it, chewed and spat out the bitter pulp. Olwen laughed.

'Are you not hungry?' he demanded.

'I am,' she admitted. 'My belly is empty.'

A while later, Quintus said, 'You know, my master will be so angry. He was told that you were beautiful but wild. I overheard him tell his generals that he would show how a Roman would tame you.'

Olwen grimaced. She asked him how many Romans would be tracking them.

Quintus said he had no idea.

'You must have some.'

'Not really,' he admitted.

'Have you never seen a band of soldiers sent off in pursuit of someone?'

Quintus shook his head.

'A hunting party?'

'I never received an invitation to a hunt. Nor pined for one. I am a slave, Olwen.'

'But you have eyes to see. And ears to hear, which I know you use.'

He smiled. 'Yes. I observe what is of relevance. Military affairs do not concern me.'

'So you cannot even guess.'

Quintus frowned. 'The smallest unit in the Roman army is a contubernium. It consists of eight legionaries.'

'Good. Well done.' Olwen considered this number. 'It seems too many just to bring me back,' she decided.

'Perhaps we need horses?'

Olwen shook her head. 'I was given my own horse on my fourteenth birthday,' she said. 'I thought of taking one from the camp. But we'd be too easy to track.'

They continued walking. Quintus saw a blackbird that seemed to have its ear to the ground. It looked like it was eavesdropping on some subterranean conversation. Olwen told him it was listening for the sound of worms.

Along a stream they saw a young grey heron stalk forward on its long thin legs. Its eyes were orange and yellow, with a black button at their centre, scrutinising whatever was visible beneath the surface of the water. As it advanced, its head rocked forward on its long neck with each step. Suddenly, opening its wings for momentum, the bird thrust its long orange bill into the stream, and with a splash withdrew, an eel wriggling between the two halves of its beak.

The eel did not submit willingly to its fate but struggled, wrapping itself around the heron's beak and neck. The heron shook its head from side to side. It stood on one leg and raised the other foot and tried to dislodge the eel with its long thin toes. The eel disentangled itself and dropped into the water. But the heron was too quick and stabbed it with its spearlike beak. Then it manipulated the eel into its mouth, and in an instant swallowed it whole.

As they walked on beside the stream, Quintus said that he had been pondering his condition.

'Many days I was so attendant upon my master, explaining his whims and opinions to others, their supplications to him, that I lost myself entirely. I was not there. I became a shell, inhabited by his mind.'

Olwen shuddered. 'I could not be a slave,' she said. 'I would kill myself. Did you expect to live your whole life as one?'

'Perhaps my master would have given me my freedom. Or I might have become a freedman after his passing.'

'Did you not hate him?'

'I did not know it but yes, I did. I know it now.'

'Instead of waiting to see what you might or might not be given, look, you have taken your freedom for yourself.'

Quintus nodded. 'I have. I will never let it go.' Yet he was still thoughtful. 'As we came through Gaul,' he told Olwen, 'a female slave tried to run away. She was caught and brought back. Soldiers gathered round. Her hands and feet were tied to the ends of four lengths of rope, the other ends each to a different horse, and left thus. The horses grazed, perusing their surroundings, taking stock of the situation. As horses do. Quite calm. But as they wished to move away and felt the resistance, as the rope was taken up, each beast became agitated. They strained against their rope, and pulled harder and harder, until the woman was torn apart and they gained some measure of release.'

'The soldiers watched this?' Olwen asked.

'They began to. Most turned away long before the end. I believe some watched the whole thing.'

'Did you?'

'No,' Quintus said. 'I did not.'

Olwen nodded. 'I think I would watch it,' she said.

In valleys with creek and lush meadow and cleared woodland there were small homesteads which they skirted, climbing up and taking wooded ridges, avoiding them so as to leave no trace of their journey amongst people, who would provide news to their pursuers more readily than tracks or scent.

He asked her how she knew so much of this country if it was ruled over by a different tribe from hers.

'Each tribe has its fort, its home,' she said. 'But the Dilovi are the strongest. We hunt and roam where we will.'

'When the Romans call you cattle thieves they are lying?'

Olwen scowled. 'My father only rustles cattle in retaliation,' she said. 'Or when he's been disrespected. Or ignored.' She enumerated justifications or causes of her father's misdeeds. 'Or taken advantage of. Or from someone who thinks they can take advantage of him. We are not common thieves, Quintus. We are people of honour.'

As they walked, Olwen sang. She said they were ballads sung by the singing bards of her tribe, or of other tribes when they gathered under truce for festivals. She did not know or had forgotten the words of many of the songs but seemed to remember the tunes, and filled in verses with humming, or la-la-la, or, Quintus suspected, with words she made up as she went along, producing nonsensical rhymes.

They passed a single large stone, embedded in the earth, as tall as they were. Upon it were carved three spirals, one above the other. A simple design but carefully made on the uneven stone. Quintus asked who had put it there, and what it meant. Olwen told him it was a Druidic glyph. She did not know what it meant, and she doubted whether many Druids now indentured would know, apart from Munatius, of course, for their creeds and doctrines would have changed since this stone was planted here, would they not?

They headed south-west through a pass and down into a wooded valley. In a short while they came out of the trees into a meadow of fading flowers and tired grasses. They had half-crossed the meadow when Olwen turned and saw the hound. She had never encountered a creature like this before. It was white, smooth-coated, with pale brown patches, and it was the size of a small pony. It had long legs, a long, lean body and a lengthy rounded snout. Its ears were pendulous and swung as it loped on its long legs around the edge of the meadow.

The hound did not run with its snout to the ground, as her father's hunting dogs did when on the trail of prey, but looked around, apparently using its eyes rather than its nose. Yet it was not looking at them. Instead it seemed to ignore them, intent upon some other expedition than their pursuit. Olwen looked at Quintus, who had also frozen in place and watched with wide open eyes.

'Roman?' she asked.

He shook his head. 'I saw one like this in Gaul.' He watched it lope all the way around the meadow. When he glanced at Olwen he saw she had raised her bow and loaded an arrow and aimed it at the hound as it ran, waiting for it to come towards her.

The hound quartered the field, then turned without stopping and traversed the meadow as it had just done but in the opposite direction, at the same steady pace. Still it seemed to be unaware of them. Or it gave the impression that to acknowledge them at all was beneath it. Or as if it reconnoitred the compass points of some higher dimension than the one they inhabited.

Olwen turned full circle, tracing the spectral hound's circumnavigation. 'It's like a ghost,' she whispered. 'A ghost dog.'

'Shoot it,' he said.

'It's too far away.'

The white hound skirted the meadow then turned off into the trees from whence it had come and disappeared in an instant, swallowed by the dark wood.

Olwen lowered the bow, removed the arrow, put it back in the quiver and flipped the bow back over her shoulder. 'Come on,' she said. 'We need to cross that stream.'

It was a rivulet that had no name, nor had it ever, unless in times long past some other race of humans or gods had inhabited this land. Had named every hill and plain and river with words long gone, sunk in the soil with their blood and their bones. She told him this as they approached the brook.

They splashed upstream as they had the Hafren and other waterways since, to break the trail of their scent. To Quintus's surprise Olwen abruptly clambered out on the same side by which they'd entered.

'I don't like having stalkers behind us,' she explained. 'Especially if they intend to kill us.' She told him that foxes often doubled back and crossed their own path behind those hunting them. It was a well-practised tactic. As if she were part fox. Perhaps she was. He nodded.

They had reached the end of the meadow. The woods extended to the water's edge and the land sloped upwards. They walked up through the trees. Their eyes became accustomed to the gloom, and Quintus lost his fear that the ghost dog would materialise in front of them.

Olwen stopped and put up a hand. Quintus's heart thudded to a halt. She turned to him and raised a finger to her ear, inviting him to listen. To pay attention. He did so. The forest had its own sound. It was not silent. There was a hum made up of insects' droning, animals' movement, birds alighting or taking off from the canopy above. As he listened, Quintus understood there was another sound. A human voice. Speaking. Off to their right. Too faint to make out the language. The voice of a man, or men.

She nodded in the direction they'd been headed and they set off again. Then, to his dismay, she swerved to the right.

He caught her arm. She stopped and turned. He leaned in to her and whispered, 'What are you doing?'

'I want to see what we are up against.'

'They'll spot us.'

Olwen shook her head. 'Hunters on the scent rarely look behind,' she whispered. 'Or up above, for that matter. Trust me.'

They walked on as before. Quintus followed assiduously, his vision attuned to see her every footprint and treading in each for fear of inadvertently snapping a twig with his weight and the noise of it reverberating through the trees.

The mixed woodland opened out, and a band of six Romans appeared ahead.

'Now you know,' Quintus whispered.

'We'll track them a little further,' she replied, and set off.

He watched her, aghast. There was no option but to follow. He caught occasional glimpses of the soldiers when Olwen paused so as not to come too close upon them. There was no sign of the white hound. When he heard the Roman shout, it seemed far too close.

'I'm going to take a shit.'

Olwen turned to Quintus. He translated.

Another voice called back: 'We'll wait for you.'

'No need. I'll catch you up.'

It was apparent from the projection of the voices that the man wishing to relieve himself was at the rear, calling ahead, and the other had turned and called back from further away. Their words, which Quintus translated for Olwen, confirmed it.

Olwen unbuckled her sword belt and handed it to him, then took the bow off her shoulder and lifted an arrow from its quiver. 'Wait here,' she said, and turned and headed in the direction from which the voice had issued.

Quintus waited obediently for no more than the count of ten, by which time his fear was indistinguishable from a terrible loneliness. He drew the sword from its scabbard, lay the belt carefully upon the ground, along with their blankets and goatskin flask, and followed in Olwen's wake. What he might do with the sword he had no idea. Drop it. Fall on it.

He soon saw her. She had the bow drawn back. He advanced further and saw that the arrow was trained on a soldier squatting on the ground, his back to her. Quintus tried not to look at the man's bare arse nor see what might issue from it. But he could hear the man groan with effort or relief.

The first arrow entered the man's back and propelled him forwards onto his knees, his head thumping against the hard ground. Olwen marched forwards as she took a second arrow from the quiver and loaded the bow. She stopped, and stood and pulled back the string. The soldier had raised himself a little off the ground, his head higher than his torso. It was as if he was straining to see over some pediment or obstacle in his way. The second arrow entered his neck. He fell forward conclusively and did not move.

Olwen ran to the dead, bare-arsed soldier and divested him of his sword and spear, and leather bag. She tried to retrieve the arrows, but both were too deeply embedded in his flesh. She turned and ran back to Quintus. When she reached him he had not moved, and could not. 'Where is the belt?' she said.

He could not speak nor take his eyes from the sight of the slain Roman. She took his hand and raised it to her mouth and bit whatever part was there. Quintus yelped, but only for a moment before controlling himself. There remained five legionaries likely still within earshot.

Olwen was already running back in the direction they had come. He overtook her and led the way to where he had left the provisions and the sword belt. He sheathed the sword and returned the belt to her.

'Here,' she said, handing him the soldier's weapons. Then she turned off to the left and ran. He followed.

They padded on in the afternoon with barely a pause. Olwen said it was growing cooler. Quintus did not reply. When they ran through a grove of oaks Olwen said she imagined Quintus must wonder why the mud was black. She told him it was from the tannin in the trees. He did not say whether he had or had not noticed.

'You must have seen how many more birds there are amongst oak trees,' she said.

Quintus said nothing.

'It is because so many mosses and lichens grow upon their bark,' Olwen said. 'Insects live in them. And birds eat insects.'

Quintus only ambled on, a step or two behind her, his head to the ground as if obliged to count every single stride.

In the evening they found a track that dipped into the earth, with banks rising on either side. Scuffed out over centuries, or millennia, by the footsteps of countless men and beasts. Hazel trees growing on the banks reached over towards their kin on the far side, forming a tunnel.

Olwen said they should make their camp there. Quintus built their fire while she sharpened her sword. In the dark the hollow way seemed like an underground lair.

In the Roman's leather bag they found dried meat, and chewed it slowly. It was not much, but chewing the dried meat, as with the stale bread of the night before, was a slow process and made the meal seem more substantial.

'Have you lost your tongue, Quintus?' Olwen asked.

He said nothing, only chewed the tough meat.

'A strange affliction for an interpreter,' she persisted.

Quintus spat out a gob of animal cartilage. 'You killed a man,' he said. 'With no compunction or remorse, it seems.'

Olwen frowned. 'We may need to kill them all,' she said.

'We?' Quintus echoed. 'I'll be no use to you, Olwen. I could not do it.'

'Then I shall do it,' she said. 'You can carry the blankets and the water flask. And build our fire. And make love with me.'

Her caresses that night were tender. Her lips were soft. Quintus did not understand how she could be so gentle, and so fierce.

He woke in the night, and knew instantly what had woken him. Animals, baying for his blood. In the darkness they were close by, almost upon him. About to savage him where he lay. He shook Olwen awake.

She told him to calm himself, the wolves were far off, one here, another there, and they were only howling to tell each other their location so they could find their kin.

'How do you know?' Quintus whispered. 'They sound like they want to eat us.'

'Wolves have two reasons to howl. This is one. The other is to warn strange wolves off their territory.' She chuckled. 'If they were hunting us, my love, we wouldn't hear them.' She snuggled up to him under the blanket and said, 'Now we are awake, I shall tell you a story.'

'Another of your ancestors?' he asked.

'Yes,' Olwen whispered. 'Listen. There once was a man, a warrior and the son of a chieftain, who travelled the land to see it for himself, to have adventures in the flower of his youth and to meet his destiny. His name was Peredur. He came to a valley, through which ran a river, and the borders of the valley were wooded, and on each side of the river were level meadows. On this side of the river he saw a flock of white sheep, and on that side a flock of black sheep. Whenever one of the white sheep bleated, one of the black sheep crossed over and became white. And when one of the black sheep bleated, one of the white sheep crossed over and became black. And he saw a tall tree beside the river, one half of which was in flames from the root to the tip, and the other half of which was green and in full leaf.

'Close by he saw a youth sitting on a mound, with two greyhounds, white-breasted and spotted, on leashes by his side. The youth was of exalted bearing, but he was sad. Peredur asked why he was sad, and he said that all his subjects and all his hunting grounds had been taken from him by a sorceress. All he had left were these two greyhounds. Peredur asked which way she had gone, the youth pointed, and Peredur rode on that way.

'By and by he came to a mountain, and on the side of it was a cromlech.'

'What is that?' Quintus asked.

'A dolmen from the old times, like those we saw, where someone was buried between standing stones with a great flat stone laid on top. But the smaller stones, and the mud between them, and the turf on top had all gone, and even the bones of the one buried were gone and now all that remained were the large stones.

'A thin man came from beneath the cromlech, mounted upon a bony horse, and both man and horse were cased in rusty armour. The man held a rusty shield and a rusty lance. At his waist he wore a rusty sword in a tatty scabbard.

'They fought. And as often as Peredur cast the man off his horse to the ground, he would jump again into the saddle. Peredur dismounted and drew his sword. Whereupon the thin man grabbed the reins of Peredur's horse and rode off, and disappeared in the fog that was on the mountain.'

In the dead of night, in the hour of the wolf, they lay and Olwen told Quintus her story. She spoke quietly, as if there were others slumbering around them whom she did not want to disturb. The quietness of her speech made it feel as if she were sharing secrets. Or not secrets exactly, but confiding something precious. For his ears only.

'So Peredur followed,' Olwen continued, 'into the thick fog. He wandered for days, unable to see further than his outstretched hand, and was lost. But eventually the sun burned off the fog and Peredur found himself in an orchard. He saw his horse tethered to an apple tree, so he went to retrieve it, but a sorceress dropped out of the tree, where she'd been hidden in its branches. She had a sword of gold and a helmet of gold and she struck out at Peredur. But he avoided her blows and drew his own sword and smote her fatally.

'Then out of all the trees in the orchard people climbed down from where they'd been trapped by the sorceress's magic. They gathered around the youth who had been their young master, and all returned together to their hunting grounds. For the rest of his life Peredur was welcome there, and when he was dispirited he would go and join his friend, hunting wild deer and boar amongst the verdant hills. And Peredur was the grandson of Taliesin.'

'Your great-great—'

'My great-great-grandfather. Many greats, yes, Quintus. We live in the time we are given, this moment, but our ancestors are here with us always. Do you not understand? And those who will come after, they are here too. Now,' she said, 'why don't you tell me of your mother?'

They lay side by side. Quintus turned to Olwen and kissed her. 'My mother was a slave,' he said. 'One of the traders had brought her to Ephesus in a shipload up the coast from Alexandria. She came from somewhere deep in the interior. "A place you won't find on any map," she used to tell us. My father saw her in the marketplace and bought her. At once he gave her her freedom, and begged her to marry him.'

'Is that true?'

'So we were told. My sister and I were scared of our mother. She was the one who chastised us. She had a leather strap with which she inflicted formal punishment. Or she might just as easily give us a sudden painful smack. Our father never even reprimanded us. Naughtiness amused

74

him. Yet it was my mother I went to when I was hurt or unhappy. Then she would clean a wound and hold me until my sobs abated. She was big. I lost myself in her. She always smelled of jasmine.'

Quintus said no more.

Olwen drew him to her and held his trembling body.

'I miss her, Olwen,' he spluttered. 'I miss her so much.'

'I love you, Quintus,' she said, as she stroked his back.

6

IN the morning they rose before dawn and set out. The
path emerged from the hollow way. Out of a glade of
silver birches it descended towards the valley of the River
Wye. Below them lay a wide green meadow, its grass covered in white lace.

'The little people have been out in the night and sewn
it,' Olwen conjectured. 'Occult seamstresses.'

'What for?' Quintus demanded.

'They are making a funeral shroud for one of the
Cornish giants.'

'A fair guess.'

'Or a bridal veil for a queen, whose train will be carried
by a hundred maids following.'

Quintus smiled. 'Your imagination is appealing to me,
Olwen,' he said.

She frowned at him and shook her head. 'It is true,'
she said.

As they came closer they saw that the sheet was made of many thousand square patches, laid side by side. Each one was a cobweb, white in the morning dew, spun in the night by tiny spiders.

They ran on, their footsteps a path of desecration across the extraordinary craftwork.

The river was wide and shallow in these last days of summer, though the flotsam of dead wood entangled in the trees on the banks was evidence of how high it must rise once the rains come. They walked north upstream and came to a crossing place, where large flat rocks had been placed as stepping stones. The water was clear, and the riverbed was composed of black stones and brown pebbles. One behind the other they made their way across.

On the far bank, Olwen picked a fading yellow flower. She told Quintus he had to blow all the petals from it in one breath.

'Why?' he asked.

'If you can do it, it means the one you love will love you.'

He took a deep breath, and blew until all the yellow petals had flown into the air.

On the western side of the river valley they climbed through high, dry bracken. When they came out at the top Olwen stopped and turned. 'Let me look at you,' she said.

She inspected Quintus's torso. 'Here,' she said, pointing to a small dark insect. It had embedded itself in his skin.

Quintus grimaced. 'Another of your creatures after my blood?'

Olwen showed him how to remove the tick by pincering it between thumb and forefinger and twisting it off. 'If you just pull you'll likely leave the head in.' Then she crushed it, staining the stone with blood. She found two more.

Then it was Quintus's turn to examine Olwen's skin. He could not resist kissing it. 'You have a birth mark here,' he said, touching her back at her waist. He kissed it too.

'Concentrate,' Olwen told him.

He removed two ticks from his lover, and using the same stones as she had stained them likewise with her blood, mingled with his, then they set off.

At Red Pass they walked beside the ruins of a small homestead. The thatched roofs had fallen in and mud walls were leaching from the latticed skeletal framework, itself now rotting in the open. Soon they passed another. Had war passed through? Plague? One they passed still had ragged people there. Were they simply inept or unfortunate farmers? Did famine strike the competent and incompetent alike? A thin dog looked more miserable than its owners.

After they had passed, Quintus asked Olwen why the dog stayed with those people who offered it no succour.

It would surely be better off looking for more proficient masters. She told him he understood nothing of loyalty, or at least less than common curs did.

Quintus saw smoke rising, a grey wisp in the blue sky, ahead of them. He nudged Olwen and gestured to the smoke. 'Yes,' she said. She did not cut off away but said, 'I'm hungry,' and kept walking.

He paused, then trotted after her.

The smoke rose from a hole in the thatched roof of a roundhouse. They walked between one corral of woven branches housing half a dozen cattle and another which was empty. The cattle had access to a drinking trough fashioned from a felled tree trunk, a furrow for the water grooved roughly out of it. In a smaller, more substantial enclosure a dark brown pig stood and raised its head and gazed at them down its long snout. Half a dozen piglets bothered it and swarmed for milk from its teats. A goat was tethered to a stake and nibbled a perfect circle of grass.

From a muck heap steam rose. In a fourth pen grew cereals and vegetables. In amongst rows of beans and peas climbing wicker tripods a young woman bent. Perhaps she heard them, or perhaps they crossed a corner of her vision, but anyhow she stood and, clutching a small hand hoe or pick in one hand, and weeds she'd just uprooted in the other, stared at them. She was plump, and red-faced from exertion or perhaps shyness. Then she closed her eyes, as if by not seeing them neither would they see her. Yet her sightless head rotated with their movement, tracking them with her ears.

Away from the roundhouse was yet another fold, this constructed of willow branches woven around ash stakes. Perhaps it was a small paddock for horses. A man wheeled a barrow from the direction of the creek that ran through the vale towards this pound, where another, younger man was using his hands to squeeze and shape a mixture of mud and straw between the woven sticks. So it was not a pound for horses but the wall of another house. The man slapped the mud into place and it spattered on his tanned, naked torso.

When he saw the strangers, the older man set down the barrow and stood and gaped as the woman in her vegetable patch had. The other man had not noticed and continued to knead and pat the damp earth in place, as if it were dough and he a baker preparing a great circular loaf of some sort peculiar to these green valleys.

Olwen made for the thatched roundhouse, from which the smoke came, as well as the aroma of food cooking. Swallows flew out from under the eaves. Before they reached the house a woman appeared in the open door-way. She appraised them, then gracefully dropped to one knee, said, 'Olwen,' and bowed her head. Small children emerged from the darkness of the roundhouse behind her. A boy; a girl; another girl. They frowned at these strangers, then studied their mother in her unusual posture. The elder girl knelt too, then the others copied her. Meanwhile the men had come over, and when they saw this tableau of genuflection they too dropped to their knees. Finally, the woman from the vegetable garden had opened her eyes and followed the red-headed warrior woman and her dark-skinned consort, and now she joined her kith and knelt. Quintus noticed now her protruding midriff.

'Stand,' Olwen said.

Rising to her feet, the woman who had recognised Olwen took charge. She invited the fugitives inside and served them stew from a cauldron. She ordered the older man to pour mead and the younger, pregnant woman to cut slices from a loaf of dark brown and barely risen heavy bread, fresh from the clay oven. She sent the children out to pick peas for their guests. The man brought them two clay goblets of mead. After he set these down he turned, and Quintus saw he carried a pack on his back. Inside was a baby, swaddled tight in a frame or board, its straps around the man's shoulders and waist. The baby peered at them with pale blue eyes.

The single room of the roundhouse was like a cavern, with the cooking pot or cauldron on the fire in the centre and sleeping frames around the perimeter. The pregnant woman crushed grains of wheat between two stones to extract flour, and the older man took their sandals and rubbed oil into the leather. The rest of the family simply sat and watched them eat. Quintus was ravenous, Olwen too. The watery stew of root vegetables contained gristly gobbets of mutton that did not reduce upon chewing but had to be swallowed entire to avoid insulting their hosts, but Olwen managed to eat slowly, elegantly, politely, one spoon at a time. Quintus took his lead from her. Unused to alcohol, it befuddled him somewhat. He was uncomfortable being observed and wished the family would join them at the meal, but Olwen did not share this awkwardness, and she did not invite them to do so.

Sitting on the floor, the children shucked the peas they had collected. The older woman spoke. 'I recognised you at once, Your Ladyship,' she said. 'My mother's cousin was a companion to your grandmother. I came to your father's coronation when I was a child and to your parents' wedding. Long before I found myself a farmer's wife, I lived at the fort on the Mallaen mountain with you all. My father was a freeman and a warrior. Perhaps my son,' she said, nodding not to the boy passing a wooden bowl of peas to the guests but to the baby in the caboose on her husband's back. 'Perhaps he will be a warrior too. So our fortunes rise and fall and rise again. Satellites of your family's court.'

The woman spoke garrulously and the others said not a word. They listened with grave attention to her discourse, as if they might learn something she had previously omitted to tell them. They sat cross-legged or on their haunches on the dry tamped-down earth that was the floor of their house and watched their guests with a wide-eyed, unsettling patience. As if these visitors were from some place they had been unsure actually existed.

Olwen asked the woman why the men were building a second roundhouse when this one was so capacious. She nodded first at her husband, then at the other woman. 'His little sister,' she said, 'wants her own accommodation. By the time her firstborn arrives. A person could be forgiven for thinking it is she with a noble's blood in her veins. But it is not.' She turned to the pregnant girl. 'Is it?' she demanded.

The sister-in-law had been watching the guests avidly even as she ground the wheat. But now with attention upon her she lowered her gaze. 'No,' she whispered.

'Speak up, girl,' the farmer's wife ordered. 'We cannot hear you.'

'No,' the girl repeated, a little louder. Quintus estimated her age to be much the same as Olwen's and his own. The young man, who had pulled a loose shirt over his muddy torso, likewise. Together they were embarked upon the act of bringing new life into the world. And getting out of the house of this harridan.

84

'And you have four children yourself?' Olwen asked. She spoke with a tone Quintus had not heard heretofore. Solicitous yet regal. Not dissimilar to his master with the troops, though she was so young.

Their hostess waved her arm to indicate other children outside, whose names and number she had forgotten or could not be bothered to specify. 'The older girl and the dog are with the sheep.'

Quintus did not notice that Olwen had left a remnant of stew, a gobbet of bread, until after he had wiped his bowl with the last of his heavy bread and eaten it. Perhaps he had committed a subtle breach of tribal etiquette. He left the remainder of his mead.

'We thank you,' Olwen said, to the woman but then looking at each member of the family in turn. 'Thank you. You have given us full bellies.' She rose, as did Quintus, and all the others climbed to their feet as fast as they could and stood in a row, attendant. It occurred to Quintus how curious they must be to how it was that a chieftain's daughter travelled through this country, alone but for the company of a foreigner. Yet none asked.

'I must warn you,' Olwen said, 'men are after us. Romans. If you tell them you gave us succour, they may kill you. Out of malice. I would advise you to use the goat to cover our tracks with its stink. If still they come here, deny that you saw us. Perhaps we came at night without your knowing. Better yet, tell them you heard of a young couple travelling close to here, heading for the hills around Water Break-its-neck to the east.'

The instructions seemed to Quintus complicated. If they had to concoct a lie, could all maintain it?

Olwen nodded, and the members of the family all bowed to her. She turned and headed for the doorway. Quintus nodded to them, and turned and followed Olwen outside. She was walking fast out of the compound. He caught her up and fell into step beside her. Seconds later they heard footsteps behind them and turned and saw the young pregnant woman lurching after them. They stopped and waited for her. She held a bag. No, not a bag but a patch of old material, its corners bunched up and grasped in her hand. She passed this to Quintus. 'For your journey,' she said.

Quintus thanked her. They resumed, and as they walked he opened up the makeshift bag and found therein two carrots, two apples and two strips of some kind of dried meat.

Every time they came into the open the view had changed, with dizzying shifts of perspective. Distant heights were gained swiftly, and just as abruptly they found themselves back in a valley floor.

They skirted a long curvilinear ridge. Quintus looked up and saw a facade of cut stones that must be the wall of a castle. Yet there was no other building there; this wall stood alone on the hill, surely the remnant or ruin of some ancient fortress. Perhaps the steep slope had been revetted with drystone walling. He pointed it out to Olwen but she said he was wrong, they were only stones. He said perhaps men had got the idea of building stone walls from just such prodigies of nature.

'But we do not build such things,' she told him.

'Are all your buildings bodged out of mud and wood?' he asked.

She ignored him and did not answer, and they dropped steeply into the Dulas river valley.

From the stone- and heather-covered summit of a hill they looked down on the confluence of the Elan and the Wye rivers, and they ran along cliffs above the Elan. A small stream had cut a deep gash in the hillside, they scrambled down and up the other side and looked through the cut across the grey slate cliffs of the Elan valley to the Cambrians, a waving line of mountains in the distance.

They ran on, down into the river valley. On the other side rose a grey rounded crag, like a slumbering stone beast. They trotted along the Rhiwnant stream beneath a long rocky bluff above them, its lower slopes littered with granite boulders. Across the Rhiwnant was a simple mud dwelling, seemingly abandoned. Some long-gone, enterprising resident had built rough stone terraces on which to grow their vegetables, like the terraces of Rome.

The Rhiwnant valley stretched away, its bare rocky hillside, dotted with tough trees and one single stand of pine, sloping towards the stream. Instead of entering it, Olwen took an arrow from her quiver and dropped it on the ground. Then she turned south and ran around the end of the crag and through a cwm. This pass had been cut by a small mountain brook, which they followed upstream beside its cascading waterfalls, up through groves of stunted oaks onto a high isolated plateau of acid grassland. Despite its elevation the soil of the open moorland was underlain by mudstone, which did not drain well, so they had to struggle through blanket bog above thick layers of peat. Then the underlying rock must have become more porous, for it was dry underfoot and they found themselves running across rough upland meadow-grass and purple willowherb.

On reaching the heights they paused to drink, and to get their breath back. The wind dried their sweat. They looked down on a buzzard circling below them. Olwen told Quintus that this was where her people brought their dead.

'You do not bury them?' he said.

'We leave them to the elements,' she said.

They looked back, as they did from every summit, each time fearing they would see their Roman pursuers. The terrain was clear.

'You left your arrow to make them think we went that way?' Quintus asked.

'Have you ever noticed,' she asked, 'if you hear a robin sing, then turn in the direction of that song, you cannot see it?'

Quintus nodded earnestly, as if this were something he had indeed noticed.

'It's because a robin has learned to throw its voice, to confuse a crow or other predator that might attack it.'

'I often wondered why it did that,' Quintus lied.

'Like the robin, I laid a false trail.'

'Maybe we've lost them,' he said.

Olwen shook her head. 'Don't fool yourself,' she said. 'But do not worry, Quintus, we'll soon be with my tribe.'

I do worry, he wanted to say. That is precisely what worries me. But he said nothing.

A golden plover assailed Olwen with its plaintive cry. She set out and they ran across the tussocky moorland then dropped down through the treeline back into woods. There were rowans and birches, and clearings in which oak trees, given space, had, like people yawning in the morning, stretched out their branches into the air over the years of their growing, luxuriant and stately. Through breaks in the trees they could see mist in the valley below. Alongside the track she had found were long puddles in which trees were reflected, though it could as well have been that the water was glass and what they were seeing were the tree roots, exact replicas of the branches above. The path followed a stream that meandered serpentine, less following the contours of the land than lazily taking its time to reach the valley floor.

In the fertile valley, there was a gathering of small roundhouses and enclosures. Olwen sensed people watching them but spotted no one, neither in the dwellings nor with the animals.

Across the Irfon was a rough plank bridge. The thin river had cut its passage between high wide bluffs and they climbed up the other side. Brown cattle grazed amongst wilting bracken.

Soon they were back in rolling wooded hills. Quintus was uneasy with what they were running from and running to, but he buried his unease in motion.

They came to a stream in a gully whose rocks and pebbles were all rusty red, but the water was clear and they filled their flask. They plodded through boggy turf and tuffety marsh grass, then up over a saddle of hills and down again. In a wide valley ahead of them, they glimpsed conical wooded mounds whose ash trees had already lost their leaves, lending the mounds the appearance of skulls of men with thinning hair. Olwen steered to her right, moving always in a certain direction, with definite purpose. Occasionally she paused and looked around, but less it seemed to Quintus to ponder which way to go than to sniff the air like a fox before resuming her journey.

Where the Tywi river came down a steep gorge, narrow and rushing towards the wide valley, they clambered over the rocks to reach the other side, then they climbed through fescue and cotton grass, and tall thistles, their purple crowns turned white with seeds. Gusts of wind blew swirling blizzards of white down before them.

Now there was a bounce to Olwen's step. 'We shall reach my home by nightfall,' she said. 'We'll be safe then.'

Quintus nodded, although he was sure that she was wrong. They jogged on. He had to say something.

Through a pass they crossed a tableland of purple heather that scratched their ankles, then dropped down through oak woods. In a clearing a flock of thirty or forty linnets, little finches, searched busily for seeds. They paused to rest beside an old, dead oak tree. Its skeleton was more or less intact, a great lantern of branches, the truncated ends like antlers. Yet from some outer branches new twigs and bushels of leaves had sprouted. It was as if the tree had died and lain dormant, defeated, then been reprieved with new tentative vitality, for one last shot at existence.

'Stop,' Quintus said.

Olwen came to rest a yard ahead of him and turned.

He shook his head. 'We cannot go to your home, Olwen. Do you know that?' He looked into her eyes. 'You must know that. Do you not?'

Olwen frowned. Did she understand what he was telling her?

'Your father will kill me,' he said. 'He will send you back to Frontinus.'

She shook her head, vigorously. Her hair ruffled and shimmered about her. It really was the rich russet red of a fox. As if she were part vulpine.

'I will explain to him,' she said. 'It was not your doing. It was mine. I will tell him.'

'He will not believe you.'

'He knows I make my own decisions.' Olwen laughed. 'He knows it well. He has complained of it all my life. He blamed my mother's leniency. While she blamed his blood.'

Quintus did not smile, but hung his head. 'He will not believe you could have done something this foolish. So injurious to his welfare.'

He glanced up and saw anger spark in her eyes like a brief crackle of lightning, then she threw herself at him. He fell backwards, the wind knocked out of him, and she was on top of him. He twisted this way and that and managed to roll her off him and raise his arms. He had hold of one of her wrists. She had hold of one of his. They wrestled in the grass. The grass stained their limbs green, twigs caught in their hair, flecks of matter stuck to their sweaty skin as they grappled furiously. Wildflower seeds flew into their mouths and they spat them off their tongues as they fought. Soil beneath and between the grass rose as dust around them. Olwen was a fighter and Quintus was not, but he was heavier than her and held his own.

He lay atop her, pinning her down, but she had her legs wrapped around his torso, trapping him. The anger was still in her eyes, but they were those of an animal unsure whether it is hunter or prey. The eyes of a cornered fox. How close to making love this was. Perhaps only lovers wrestled quite like this.

Quintus felt the grip of Olwen's legs go slack; her hold on his wrist loosened. She closed her eyes. He waited. When she opened them again the anger was gone, replaced by tears.

'I know,' she said. 'I know.'

Quintus climbed off her, she raised herself up, and he embraced her.

'I can't go back,' Olwen said. 'I can never go back.'

A wind from the north had picked up through the afternoon. It blustered around rocks and rustled leaves in the trees. In a covert of buckthorn and hazel Olwen spotted a young deer. She laid a hand on Quintus's arm. He stood and watched her slowly take the bow over her shoulder and load it with an arrow from the quiver.

She stood side-on to the animal nibbling grass, and slowly raised her bow. The fawn moved as it grazed, from one mouthful of fodder to the next, and edged around a tree. If it thought to evade the hunter it could not have made a better plan. It inched out of shot. Quintus looked across and saw that Olwen had drawn back the arrow a little. He watched as she held it there. He glanced towards the tree and saw the fawn's head emerging slowly on the other side. When he looked back at Olwen, she had drawn the arrow fully back, the feathers now grazing her chin, yet she had done it so slowly he had not seen it happening.

The bow was bent and the string of the bow was tense. The deer grazed, oblivious, and moved into full view. Suddenly Olwen tugged the string back a last inch, as far as she could, then let go, all in a split second. Quintus did not see the arrow fly, but looked towards the deer and saw it stagger and fall.

Olwen crudely butchered the animal with her sword, hacking at the warm meat. They ate the liver and the kidneys raw, and the heart, and packed rump steaks in the bag to roast later. As they walked away, Quintus asked if the carcass would not help their pursuers track them.

'Other animals will aid us,' she said. 'We have provided them with food they do not need to catch.'

They heard a scuffle behind them and turned to see a black bird descend awkwardly through the canopy and land beside the feast laid before it.

The air was busy with midges. Swallows came and went hawking low over the land. Nightjars hunted for moths in the dusk.

Olwen stopped and said, 'Follow me.' She climbed a tree. Quintus scurried after her, his heart beating. Had she heard the soldiers close behind them?

'Watch,' she whispered.

There was a sandy mound below them, off to one side. Quintus saw there were holes of some kind, openings, in this hummock. Suddenly a black-and-white-striped face rose out of the mouth of its den. It stopped, dropped back, rose again and sniffed. Sifting the air for scent of danger.

They sat in the tree, above the badger's range of smell. Soon after, cubs followed their parent out of the sett and Olwen and Quintus watched them play. They rolled and tumbled together. There were four of them.

'What strange beasts they are,' Quintus whispered.

Olwen told him that badgers wreck wasps' nests in autumn, to consume the grubs. They eat mostly earthworms and plants. Tubers, bulbs, grass. But they are perfectly happy to kill and eat the young of rabbits' nests or foxes' dens. They even kill hedgehogs, she said, and gnaw them out of their quilled jackets.

Below them, the badger family wandered off. Olwen climbed down out of the tree, and Quintus clambered after her.

The night was cold. Quintus built a compact fire. He skewered cuts of deer meat and set the skewers across the flames, resting on stones either side. Olwen honed her sword.

Quintus put his hand on Olwen's arm to pause her. 'What is that sound?' he asked.

Olwen stopped and listened. 'What sound?'

'Those high-pitched cries,' he said, and looked up.

Olwen too looked up, and saw the pipistrelle bats veering across the darkening sky, hunting midges and mosquitoes. 'You can still hear them? I don't seem to be able to any more,' she said. 'I must be growing older quicker than you.'

They ate. Then, their bellies full, their mouths redolent of the venison, they kissed for a long time. They made love slowly, intently, their ardour increasing until Quintus could no longer stand it and came to a conclusion. Afterwards, he caressed Olwen's skin. He found by touch a small scar on her left upper arm, another on her thigh, a third on her back.

'How come you learned to fight?' he asked.

'My foster brothers taught me. Or you might say I taught myself, in order to avoid their blows.'

'Did your father allow this?'

'Why would he disallow it? There have always been women who preferred the hunt to the garden. Iron weapons to sewing needles.'

Quintus murmured his understanding. 'Ephesus was named after a warrior queen, Ephesia. And our most precious temple was that of Artemis.'

'Who was she?'

'A goddess of the hunt.'

Olwen told him that her foster brothers called her the lynx. Quintus asked her why that was.

'I fought patiently. Slowly. Then quick, to strike like a lynx. With surprise. The others tried to intimidate their opponent. Terrify them, with grimaces and screams.'

'You did not?'

She smiled. 'Sometimes I might. My own brother had neither interest in nor aptitude for masculine pursuits. Hunting, horse racing, fighting. He preferred to stay at home with our mother. Cooking. He is a fine cook. We think he may become a Druid.'

'You exchanged roles?'

'My father needed a successor. He thought I would do.'

'How did he change his mind, to give you to Frontinus?'

Olwen scratched her head through her lustrous hair. 'I told you that farmers do not fight. They bring their produce to market. Traders travel, they buy and sell. My father could see that fighting is disruptive to this economy. Much of the forest has been cleared. Our farmers grow emmer and spelt, wheat and barley, in the lowlands. In the uplands they graze their sheep and cattle. In his heart my father is a warrior, but in his head he believes that the warring tribes belong to a past age. And now the Romans are here too.'

Quintus began to say more, but Olwen interrupted.

'I will tell you another story about my great-great-grandfather, Peredur, from those wandering days of his youth. Listen. He came to a hill, and on the hill was a mighty fort. He struck the gate with his lance, and a lean auburn-haired boy appeared on the ramparts, and saw him, and came down and opened the gate. When he went into the roundhouse, Peredur beheld eighteen youths, lean and red-headed, like the one who had let him in.

'They were courteous, they disarrayed him of his cloak, and they sat down to discourse. Thereupon five maidens came into the house. Peredur was certain he had never seen one as fair as the fairest of the maidens. She had an old garment of satin upon her, once handsome but now so tattered that her skin could be seen through it. White was her skin, her eyes were green as malachite, and her hair was red and full and fell over her shoulders.'

'Ha!' said Quintus. 'I know how this story goes.'

'How could you?'

'This must be your great-great-grandmother-to-be, for this could be a description of you yourself.'

'Don't be stupid, Quintus. And don't interrupt. The maiden welcomed Peredur and invited him to eat. Food was brought, and a flask of wine. Peredur heard the servant tell the maiden that this was the last of it. When it was time for them to sleep, a tent was prepared for Peredur, and he went to rest.

'"Behold, sister," said the youths to the fairest maiden, "we have counsel for you. Go to your guest, who has the air of a great warrior, and offer to become his wife."

'"How can you recommend this?" she answered. "I have not been the lady love of any warrior, and to make him such an offer before I am wooed by him, truly, can I not."

'"Unless you do this," they said, "we will leave you here to your enemies, to do as they will with you."

'And so this maiden went forth shedding tears to Peredur. He awoke and said, "Tell me, sister, why do you weep?"

'She told him how her father had possessed these dominions. Then the son of the chief of another tribe came to ask him for her hand. She was not willing, and her father would not give her, either to him or to any other, against her will. She was her father's only child. In time her father died, and still she rejected the rival, whose own father had died and who was now the chief of his tribe. So he declared war against her, that he might win her by force.

"'He has conquered my possessions except this one hill fort," she told Peredur, "which has been defended by my cousins, who you have met. But now we are out of provisions, and his army is upon us, and they will attack us any day. And so I am come to place myself in your hands, that you might save me by taking me hence or by defending me here, whichever may seem best to you."

"'Go, my sister," said Peredur, "and sleep. I shall defend you as best I can."

'In the morning he went out, and saw this chieftain's army arrayed in the field before the fort. He took his horse and rode down the hill, and sought the chieftain, and challenged him to combat. This man came out, mounted on a spirited black snorting palfrey that advanced at a prancing pace, proudly stepping. And they fought in the field, surrounded by the chieftain's army, but neither could prevail.

'Then they fought on foot with their swords until their aims struck sparks of fire like stars from one another, and thus they continued fighting until blood and sweat obscured the light from their eyes. Then Peredur remembered the maiden for whom he fought, and he was roused and called to himself all his strength. He raised his sword and struck the chieftain upon the crown of his head, and overthrew him. The chieftain begged for mercy. "You will have mercy," said Peredur, "if you restore to the maiden all her possessions, and give her arms, and horses, and meat and drink to last for many months, and go back to your own kingdom." So it was.'

'And Peredur stayed with her?' Quintus asked.

'At first he went on,' Olwen continued, 'for these were the days of his wandering. One day he entered a valley, and came to a hermit's cell. The hermit welcomed him, and bade him spend the night in his cave. In the morning he was woken by a tapping sound. He arose, and went out, and saw a woodpecker at a tree nearby. It seemed to him that the bird was there for his observation. He thought of the fair maiden he had saved. Her skin was like that of the woodpecker's chest, her eyes were like those of its green feathers, her hair was red as its bright crest. He turned his horse, and rode back to that hill fort. And yes, you are right, Quintus, she was my great-great-grandmother. Her name was Rhiannon. She welcomed him, and so they married. His days of wandering were over.'

They lay beside each other. Neither spoke. Quintus did not ask Olwen why she cried, but held her until her sobs abated. Then she said, 'Your turn, my love. Tell me of your sister.'

'My sister, yes,' Quintus repeated. 'Yes, I will. My parents tried for years to have children. When they gave up,

I appeared. A year later, my sister turned up too. I was their miracle, she was mine. We were each other's best friend. Everything new we encountered together. It meant she was precocious, but I was protective of her. She had to stay at home and help our mother, learn womanly skills, but whenever she could she came with me and we ran our father's errands together. She wasn't as fast a runner as me, and I was short with her, and then I felt bad afterwards.

'She was lighter-skinned than me. She had big brown eyes. Not even our mother could be annoyed with her for long. "If you take me to the hippodrome, Quintus," she'd say, "I'll play chess with you later." I think she would have been the one to take over from our father, a natural merchant.'

'And you would have run errands for her?' Olwen asked.

'I was already enthralled by the different languages I heard issue from the mouths of men. It was fascinating to me. It was music. I begged them to translate the words they used for familiar things. Some indulged this irritating boy. My father would present me to a foreign client, whom I'd greet in his own tongue, like a performing animal.

'My sister and I would walk home hand in hand, planning our business together, proud of each other's peculiar talent, impatient for the end of childhood, still many years distant.'

'I never had a sister,' Olwen whispered. 'Only now, listening to you speak of yours, do I miss having one.'

'I never had a brother,' Quintus said. 'When we have children, we shall need to have at least four, if every one is to have both a brother and a sister.'

Olwen did not reply, and she did not laugh out loud, but Quintus could feel her ribs jiggling and her breast nudging against him.

7

T HE darkness drained upwards, off the horizon, and it was followed by colour, fierce pink paint daubed across the horizon by some hot impatient hand.

Quintus prepared to set off. 'Wait,' said Olwen. She led him back to the badgers' sett.

'Are they not back inside now?' he asked. 'Nocturnal animals, sleeping?'

Olwen climbed the slope above the sett and lay on the ground, her ear to the earth. 'Listen,' she said.

Quintus too lay, and heard the bumps and rumbles of the badger cubs, still playing, roistering about underground.

They walked the cold night out of their bones through dying nettles, drooping hollyhocks and foxgloves. The wild roses had faded and the red rose hips glowed bright in scrubland.

Periodically Quintus's attention was drawn to the grey

sky; whenever he looked up there were birds, flying south. Different species. In ones and twos or in flocks of great number. Those like geese, with long necks straining forward. It was as if they were all fleeing some catastrophe, only visible from above.

It was lazy to say the sky was grey. 'I do not believe,' he told Olwen, 'there can be a language yet devised with enough words to convey all the shades of grey I see in your Welsh sky.'

Olwen told him they did not need words; colours were their own vocabulary, and we only had to see keenly and our eyes understood.

In a forest, hazel leaves were falling, though the oaks were still green. They walked through a holt of beech trees, whose yellow leaves yielded to each breeze and fluttered over them. As if at a ceremony of their union. And they were both a little abashed, awkward with each other, until Quintus laughed. 'The trees approve of us.'

Olwen said it was indeed a consecration. Quintus took her hand, and they held hands as they walked. And the leaves on the ground were like a golden carpet laid for them.

They came out of the autumnal forest into a long barren valley of granite scree and boulders, its only growth scattered thorn trees. The sky was black in the west. A brisk cold wind rippled over them and made them shiver. The black cloud spread like ink. A flock of doves raced before the storm, eastward. Deer cantered across the valley up ahead, bolting for cover.

'Perhaps it will pass by us,' Quintus said.

'Perhaps it won't,' Olwen said. 'Can you not smell it?'

'I don't think so.'

The dark cloud loomed over them, and the day darkened. 'Can you taste it, though? It tastes like iron. On your tongue?'

'I think I can hear it,' Quintus said.

'Look you,' Olwen said. 'Here it comes.'

The rain drummed towards them and then fell with trenchant force, drenching them in seconds. Their hair was lank, their clothing sodden. Then as quickly as it came the cloud passed over them. The rain ceased. The sun appeared. The cool air had been washed clean. Their clothing dried out slowly as they trudged on, shivering.

They followed the Melyn stream into the Cothi valley, and into woodland below an escarpment of dark rock.

A hare sat up on its haunches and watched them pass less than a dozen paces away. A moment later they surprised a young deer. The creature did not scamper off: it continued blithely grazing on the scant autumnal grass. Birds did not fly away but alighted on branches in their path, as if to introduce themselves to these young human visitors passing by.

Quintus remarked on the tameness of the animals.

'We've entered the grove,' Olwen told him.

Quintus noticed shapes carved into the trunks of trees. Here a rough decorative pattern, there the crude likeness of a bearded man. Or of a horse. They seemed like sculptural sketches. Artistic rehearsals. Hanging from branches were twigs tied together, or pieces of wood fashioned into odd configurations, floating in space. Some were not wood but bone. Parts of a skeleton. One animal or another. A human skull hung on woven string.

Olwen led the way, and in a glade she found the shaman. The one who had accompanied her to the Roman camp. He was dressed in threadbare clothes, with rags on his feet. His hair was straggly, his beard unkempt. He was seated on a log and appeared to be deep in conversation with a young ram. He spoke and the sheep listened. As if to instruction, perhaps, or to confession. When they came closer they saw that the Druid was uttering endearments as to a pet, and the sheep attended, for the man was scratching its chin and it stood mute in rapt motionless delight.

When he saw Olwen, the Druid rose and embraced her. 'My child,' he said. He had tears in his eyes. 'Shameless, wilful, poor dear girl.'

He bade them come sit as if in his tent or roundhouse, though it was merely a small clearing in a wood. Olwen found a log close to the Druid, but there was no other, so Quintus sat cross-legged on the ground.

'I wish I could offer you a hearty meal,' the Druid said. 'That lad is supposed to cook for us, but when he is lost in woodcarving he forgets our feeble bodies require nourishment.' He turned around. 'Veldicca!' he yelled. Then he turned back. 'He won't hear me.'

Olwen told him all that had happened since he had blessed her at the Roman camp. 'I know we cannot go home,' she said. 'I don't know where to go.'

'You came to me.'

'I don't know what to do.'

The Druid raised his head and gazed up into the tops of the trees around them, as if some solution to this girl's plight might show itself. He lowered his head. 'Perhaps your life is over,' he said. 'When you fled, it was the completion of what you were fated to do. All this' – the shaman raised his hands, open wide, and waggled them to and fro to indicate everything around them – 'this aftermath, is like the trail left by a shooting star in the night sky.'

'Can you not tell me what to do, Munatius?' she pleaded.

The shaman threw back his head and cackled. 'Look at this body,' he said, 'this sack of offal and blood. With two legs to prance about on and a head full of nothing, yet equipped with a tongue to articulate that nothing to others. What use am I?'

'My father esteems you, Munatius.'

'Your father? Thank you, child. Kind words. If he discovers I am sheltering you, he will cut my throat himself.' The Druid gestured over his shoulder, in the direction of the hill fort. 'Right now he is trying to decide whether to attack the Romans, mount defence against their onslaught, or flee to the northern mountains.' The Druid nodded as if agreeing with what he'd just heard, though it had come from his own mouth. 'Perhaps my apprentice would inform on me. I don't doubt he believes himself ready to take over my role. I have shared with him most all I know, and he knows some other things of his own.' Again he yelled for Veldicca.

'My father would not execute you, Munatius. You are of the highest value to him.'

'I was not thinking of myself alone. I was wondering what use we are.'

'All of us?'

'Any of us.'

Quintus spoke up. 'And what is the answer? What is our use in this world?'

'The great question,' Munatius said, still, it seemed, addressing Olwen. 'The only one. Your Roman asks it. I have not spoken with one before.'

'Do you not have an answer?' Quintus persisted.

'We had a bard, once upon a time,' the Druid said. 'Long ago. His name was Taliesin. He had a gift. When he was young he came to me.'

'To you?' Quintus interrupted.

'Yes. Or one like me. With his verses. He spoke them and requested a response. How did his words fall into another's mind? In order to improve them, you see. I told him. I know I helped him, yet I did not give him anything. You understand? I did not tell him anything he could not know. I helped him to hear his own words with his own ears.'

The three of them sat in silence. The ram had wandered off. A hen pecked for grubs or grit around Quintus's feet. A goose waddled into the glade.

'We are here to appraise God's work?' Quintus ventured.

'For some reason God requires us to fulfil the same kind of role for her, yes, I think so. Perhaps. So she can see her creation with her own eyes.' He stopped and gave due consideration to what he'd just said. He seemed to have surprised himself with the acuity or novelty of his insight.

They heard footsteps, and the young man Quintus had observed assist the Druid at the Roman camp appeared. He was dressed in a long, unwashed woollen cloak. His long hair was gathered above his head, pegged carelessly in place with twigs, and there were traces of black ink around his eyes. When he saw Olwen he blanched, then collected himself and went down on one knee before her.

'Veldicca,' the Druid said, 'would you find our guests some of your delicious food?'

The apprentice rose and nodded to each of them in turn, then walked away.

'I have heard,' Munatius said, addressing Quintus, 'that you Romans worship many deities.'

'They have many gods, yes. Mercury, Jupiter, Minerva. Countless others. Mars.'

The Druid nodded. 'There are many spirits.'

'Spirits are not gods,' Quintus said. 'The Romans have many gods.'

'There are many spirits,' the Druid repeated. 'There is only one God. Perhaps she takes different forms, for it is impossible for most men to see her as she is. So they see what they are able to.'

'Do you see God as she is?' Quintus asked.

The Druid laughed. It was a bitter sound. 'As if I could. I have spoken with many spirits. I speak with them all the time. Do you know how many there are? No, you cannot imagine. I am not too proud to ask them to intercede for me. For one of ours. But they do not, it seems. Or if they do, God ignores them. Has this girl not told you of these things?'

Sharpening her sword, Olwen had been unusually reticent. 'I have told him,' she said, 'all he needs to know. That each animate entity has its own spirit.'

'Do you see these spirits?' Quintus asked the shaman.

He shrugged and rolled his head from one side to the other, as if to suggest that he saw some, not all. 'I drink the mushroom tea each morning.'

'Munatius lives half in this world,' Olwen explained, 'half in the other.'

'A dream world?'

'Visions are not dreams,' the Druid said. 'Not quite. Not exactly. No. Though both seem random. Inexplicable to all but those who dedicate their lives to their deciphering.'

'One such as you,' Quintus said.

The shaman nodded in a way that suggested this was his burden. 'Life is life,' he said. 'We are given one each. It is easy to skate across the surface, like children on a frozen pond. It is pleasant enough to do so. Or one can break the ice, kneel perilously at its edge, and peer into the depths.' He put his palms together and raised them. 'Even dive into the dark, freezing water.'

The apprentice reappeared, bearing a slab of wood, a rudimentary tray, on which were rough wooden bowls. Veldicca held the tray before Olwen. She took a handful of shelled hazelnuts from one bowl, walnuts from another, blackberries from a third. He offered the tray likewise to the Druid, and then to Quintus. 'I carved these bowls myself,' Veldicca told him.

The bowls were of pitifully poor craftsmanship, with no decoration, plain, misshapen. Quintus could not imagine anyone in Ephesus or Rome admitting to having made them.

'He has constructed his own treadle lathe,' Munatius said. 'With his foot he activates a mechanism that turns a block of wood, so he merely holds the carving tool in place and gouges out the centre. The bowls need more practice, but the lathe is what we're proud of.'

Quintus wondered if the shaman's assistant was simple. Or if the effect of mushroom tea was overpowering for a young man.

'In the morning he will show you the tree trunk he has carved, won't you, Veldicca? Now, will you milk some beast or other? Our guests are thirsty.'

After they had drunk warm sheep's milk, Veldicca fetched a long pole with a crude crook tightly strapped to its end, with which he pulled down wood from above. High broken branches that had caught in those below them. 'Dry, see?' he said. 'Burn better.'

'Another of his inventions,' Munatius said, in the tone of a proud father.

When it came time to sleep they were not taken any-where but lay down in that glade. Veldicca brought them frayed blankets to add to their own. He built a fire and lit it. It roared and blazed bright, giving off much heat, and soon died. In the night Olwen and Quintus sidled closer and closer and slept spooned tight together. When Quintus woke, his hip and shoulder aching, and pulled apart to turn onto his other side on the hard ground, Olwen turned in her sleep too and nestled once more against him.

Quintus dreamed he was keeping watch on a great plain. There was a hurst of oak trees in the distance. In the dream he nodded off, and when he awoke with a start the wood had come closer. He scrutinised it, but nothing moved, and he fell asleep again. Again he woke to find the wood was nearer. He had to tell Olwen they must run, but in the dream she slept so peacefully and he was loath to wake her.

In the morning when they stirred they found the glade shared with other residents. Fowl roosted on a branch. A cat lay curled up beside the Druid. A calf grazed.

Veldicca was not there but appeared soon with more bowls of nuts and berries. He had goblets of some foul-smelling liquid. When offered it, Olwen declined. Quintus echoed her abstention. The shaman and his apprentice emptied a full goblet each.

Olwen sharpened her sword with the stone. Quintus asked Veldicca if he might see this totem he had made.

'I did not make it,' the apprentice Druid said, climbing to his feet. 'The totem pole is not the tree I carved.'

'Where is it?' Quintus asked, standing too.

'I do not know. It no longer exists. It existed only while I was carving it. Yesterday I finished. It disappeared.' Veldicca turned and walked out of the glade. Quintus followed. 'The dead tree is there, but not the totem pole. It will only exist when you look at it.'

Quintus said nothing.

'When you ponder it,' the apprentice continued, 'that is where it exists. In your mind. Then the trinity of collaboration is complete between myself, the tree and you. My carving was a performance, Roman. You will bring it alive again in your mind. That is it. I can say no more.'

'I understand,' Quintus said. 'I think.'

Veldicca came to a stop. 'You say you understand, yet you have walked right past it.' He sounded both aggrieved and regretful. He took Quintus by the shoulders and turned him, and pointed.

A few paces away, there it was, the trunk of a tree shorn of its branches and most of its bark. Into it were carved a multitude of faces. All were of distinct individuals, rendered with unworldly skill. Quintus walked around the pole, studying the carvings. Between the heads were minute representations of weapons, tools, animals. It appeared that a story was being told.

Veldicca said that indeed it was the story of the royal house of their tribe. The faces at the bottom were those of Peredur and his wife Rhiannon. The apprentice named those of succeeding generations as they rose above. The top of the tree had been cut off at a height a little over their heads. Veldicca pointed out Olwen's father, Cunicatus, and her mother, Alys. Above them was Olwen, clear to see. Quintus walked around the tree and came face to face with himself. The likeness was uncanny, from his lips to his curly hair. How was this possible?

At the top of the pole above Olwen and Quintus was the final head. It was that of a child.

Munatius told them he had asked for a vision and received one. A great ship was anchored in the ocean. A small boat floated towards it from the shore. A man rowed. Two figures sat, their backs to the land they were leaving.

Olwen asked the Druid what he thought would happen. Was what she had done about to bring down ruin upon her people?

The Druid reached forward and took the girl's head in his bony hands. 'Do not blame yourself,' he said. 'Our people love fighting.' He let go of her and turned to Quintus. 'The people of Wales. They always have. There was a race of giants here once, who fought each other endlessly and wiped themselves out.' The Druid leaned close to Quintus. He seemed to want to ensure that the foreign youth understood the people he now moved among. 'There were troglodytes in the caves of our hills, goblins in the valleys. Wood sprites in the forest. All belligerent, pugnacious. They eradicated each other.'

'Will this generation do the same, then?' Quintus asked.

'As long as others come here we may unify to fight them. If they leave we will fight one another again.' He bent down and picked up a maple leaf, one amongst countless fallen from a tree close by and offering an array of colours from green through yellow to crimson. The one he showed them was a deep red. 'This land,' he said, 'has been composted with the hot blood of our ancestors. The trouble is that we have believed too long that the soul is immortal. After the death of the body it may rest a while in the other world, but then it migrates to a new body. This is what my brethren have always taught. I wonder if they were wrong.'

The shaman hugged Olwen.

'Go forth and meet your destiny, child. It awaits you.'

He embraced Quintus too.

'It is important that you know what you are doing,' he said. 'Notwithstanding your love of this young woman, which of course transcends all else.'

Quintus turned to say farewell to Veldicca, but the apprentice was distracted, gazing into the trees where nothing in particular seemed to be.

Olwen took Quintus's hand, and they walked out of the glade.

8

T HEY walked through the meadows of the Cothi river valley. Olwen pointed at an alder tree, and Quintus saw the bright red crown of a small woodpecker, creeping along a branch, looking for food. A thrush ate rowan berries. Moss-covered trees shed their leaves, which floated downstream and caught in branches that hung low to the water. A full moon hung motionless in the blue sky. It appeared paused, as if the machinery of movement in the heavens had been stilled. It occurred to Quintus that perhaps the creator of the world had not completed their work then sat in observation or judgement over it, or moved on across the firmament to animate other worlds, but was obliged to recreate it every day.

When Quintus shared this rare insight with Olwen, she only shrugged and said, 'Yes. Maybe,' as if she and surely everyone else had considered and dismissed such inanities.

———

Quintus felt Olwen tap on his arm and looked up to see a bird flapping its wings furiously, as if outraged by something it saw on the ground below.

'Kestrel,' Olwen said. 'It is hovering above its prey. Watch it drop. It is something to watch. Like a stone.'

They stood observing the small falcon. Olwen said it was a female. Males were a little smaller, their heads were slate grey, and in her opinion they tended to be more beautiful than the female. They ate small rodents but other things too. Even bats. 'Keep your eyes on it,' she said. 'Don't blink, Quintus.'

Then the kestrel abruptly gave up, or changed its mind, its wings subsided, and it rose, turning, and with a shrill call flew away.

Olwen shrugged. 'They do as they wish.' She set forth. Quintus followed.

Geese flew overhead, honking, in arrowhead formation, the morning sun shining on their undersides.

'How do they choose who flies at the tip?' Quintus mused. 'Their leader?'

Olwen smiled. 'They do not think as we do,' she said. 'Do you know where they are flying to?'

Quintus shook his head.

'Birds and geese fly to an island out in the ocean. Munatius told me it was to spend the winter praying to their avian god, but I think he might have made that up. I was very young. No one knows where it is, this island.'

'You believe it exists although no one has seen it? Ever?'

'Some. Fishermen lost. But they could not show anyone the way back there. You know why not?'

'I do not.'

'The birds pecked out their eyes!'

Quintus frowned. 'How did they manage to return home and tell of this terror if they were blind?'

'They drifted,' Olwen answered, without hesitation. 'Favourable currents carried them home. Of course, many more must have suffered a similar fate but perished at sea. It stands to reason.'

Quintus gazed at her. She looked back at him. He wondered if she made these things up, improvising as she went along. He asked her if she had ever seen the ocean.

Olwen said she had not.

'Don't look so sad,' he told her. 'No doubt you will one day. You have that pleasure to look forward to.'

'You have seen many oceans, I suppose.'

'I grew up beside the sea. My friends and I were in and out of the water. I made a snorkel from a reed and swam underwater. You see a whole amazing world then, of brightly coloured fish and turtles and crabs.' He pondered. 'The sea around this island is grey, and cold, perhaps it is not for swimming in. Where I grew up the water was warm and blue.'

He told her that there were those on the east side of Ephesus who had lived their whole lives in the city yet never seen the sea. She asked how that was possible. What was a city anyhow? How many people lived there?

Quintus explained that hundreds of thousands of people lived in Ephesus. Not half as many as lived in Rome, of course. A city was like a town, but bigger.

'What is a town?' Olwen asked.

Quintus attempted to describe the mass of people that constituted an urban conurbation, but Olwen refused to believe it. She could not imagine so many people living in close proximity.

'They would kill one another,' she decided.

They slipped past a small settlement, where Olwen fingered the torc around her neck and told Quintus that the gold from which it was made had come from hereabouts. He said Frontinus would be keen to know that. They crossed a stream and passed sheep grazing in small fields with clumps of reed sweetgrass in amongst the meagre pasture, and passed a farm into more low-lying, rolling land. They crossed a footbridge spanning the Marlais brook.

A crow, perched precariously on the top of a leafless hazel shoot, admonished them. Olwen cawed back at it in perfect imitation. The crow shook its head, seemingly affronted. It set its beady black eyes on Olwen and squawked at her. She smiled and screeched back at it, and it came to Quintus that she did not observe the bird, and other creatures, as he did, from a human perspective outside their realm. No, she and they inhabited the same realm, from which he was excluded.

'There are always animals watching us,' Quintus said.

'Of course. What do you expect?'

'It is as if we are passed from one creature to the next. They invigilate our journey, and pass the information on to some higher authority.'

Olwen smiled. 'How are you so ignorant of animals?' she asked.

'I was well acquainted with rats,' he said. 'They were always after the grain stores.'

'Rats?'

'You have them here. But they are red, with lots of fur, and their tails are bushy.'

'Squirrels,' she said.

They avoided further farmsteads, fording an unnamed stream and climbing into woodland with limes and whitebeams.

Olwen and Quintus saw them before they were seen, for the quartet of young men were clearly intent upon each other. They came lurching and sauntering along the narrow forest path, loudly bantering between themselves. Each held a bow, and carried a quiver of arrows slung over his shoulder and a short knife sheathed on a belt about his waist. They were similarly attired in woollen jerkins and chequered trousers, though each wore a different coloured cap on his head, rakishly or woozily askew. They reminded Quintus at once of the young men, sons of merchants, who hung around the harbour at Ephesus, in the cafes and hammams. The ones his father referred to as wastrels, good-for-nothings, something he would not countenance his own son becoming.

One youth was shorter than the others and seemed to be the butt of some raucous humour. The tallest youth issued terse quips, accompanied by comical poses, and the other two cackled delightedly while the first lad remained morose.

The hunting party noticed Olwen and Quintus approach one after another, coming to a gradual standstill, the tall one holding his arms out to either side to halt his companions. Another blinked at them, perhaps trying to bring them into focus. The tall one was the first to gather his wits and said loudly, 'Well, what have we here then?'

Quintus and Olwen came to within a few yards. 'Make way,' Olwen said.

One of the youths leaned to the tall one and whispered in his ear. His glassy eyes widened in response and he said, 'Of course. I knew I knew her.' He stepped forward. 'I'll be flayed alive if it's not Olwen, daughter of the great Cunicatus,' he slurred, in a sarcastic tone. 'Not a bad-looking maid for the scion of such a monster.'

'How dare you,' Olwen said. Quintus saw her eyes narrow. 'Step aside at once.'

The tall youth turned to his companions, grinning. 'I think perhaps we shall not, will we, boys?' He turned back to Olwen. 'Not before you and I find some soft grass beyond those rowan trees.'

The young men paid no attention to Quintus. It was as if he were invisible to them.

'If you touch one hair on my head,' Olwen said, 'my father will hunt down each one of you. He will have you disembowelled in front of your families. And then he will do the same to every last one of them. Starting with the eldest, and ending with the youngest.'

The tall youth found this prospect hilarious, and so did the other three. One performed a caricature of terror, to further laughter. Quintus glanced at Olwen and could see the colour rising in her neck. Her face reddening. The young men were ill-equipped for close combat, so their number was not so great an advantage. He saw her left hand grip tighter the scabbard of her sword.

Abruptly the tall one stopped laughing and scowled instead. 'Have you not heard?' he asked. 'The Romans march on the Dilovi camp. Your father's days are numbered. And good riddance. He humiliated my father.' He opened both his arms wide. 'And many others, all around.'

The one who had whispered to his leader earlier now did the same again. He had to rise up slightly on tiptoe to do so, and Quintus noticed that he, indeed all of them, wore woollen socks in bright colours beneath his sandals.

The tall one listened and nodded, while not taking his eyes off Olwen. Then he said to her, 'We'll let you by, maid. All you need do is defer to me, like my father did to yours.'

Quintus breathed out with relief, for all she had to do was say a word or two and they could be on their way. Instead he saw her back straighten. She grew taller and raised her chin. 'You are one of the sons of Bedwyn,' she said. 'I don't even remember which one. You are all as worthless as he was.'

Now anger twisted the youth's countenance. 'Kneel before me, you bitch, or I'll—'

Quintus held up his hand. The tall youth stopped speaking, perhaps shocked that Olwen's inanimate escort had come to life. Now Quintus whispered in Olwen's ear. 'Let us submit before these people, and move on.'

'Never,' she said.

'This is stupid,' Quintus told her. 'There's no need for blood to be spilled here.'

Olwen turned to him. Her eyes were opaque. Her expression was calm. She was no longer angry. Amused, perhaps.

'We could die here for nothing,' Quintus whispered.

Olwen smiled. 'Then let us die. Our tribes have been at war for generations. You think I would betray my grandparents? I will never kneel before him.'

Quintus understood that nothing he could say was going to change her mind. But perhaps the young man might be more biddable. 'Stay there,' he whispered. 'Don't move.' He turned to the four men and advanced towards them. Then he stopped, turned back to Olwen and barked at her in Latin. He turned on his heel and came on. 'Lads,' he said. He veered off the path, gesturing for them to step off it with him for privacy. For covert discourse.

Looking back warily at Olwen, the tall youth stepped away with Quintus. His companions followed his lead. Quintus stood with his back to Olwen and beckoned to the men that they array themselves before him, and lean in, that he might speak with them in confidence.

'Yes,' he said quietly. 'Your intelligence is accurate. The Romans march on Cunicatus. They will defeat his tribe, but then they intend to subdue all others in these western hills. I have been sent ahead to find men, brave young warriors, who can lead their tribes in concert with the Romans and thus evade the slaughter. Young gallants like yourselves.'

The short youth frowned and said, 'Why do you travel with her?' The lad stood so close Quintus smelled the alcohol on his breath as he spoke.

'Ignore her arrogance,' Quintus said. 'She is merely my travelling guide. Take pity on her. What are your names?'

They told him and he said he would relay these to the Roman governor. They were just the kind of youthful champions their people needed in the times to come. He raised a finger to his lips. 'Tell no one of our arrangement,' he said. 'People can get jealous, can they not?'

The tall youth nodded in agreement with this sage observation. Perhaps he had suffered such jealousy in the past.

Quintus turned to Olwen, who stood by in a posture of irritated impatience, and yelled at her once again in Latin. Then he added, 'Come,' and beckoned her forward. The four youths at the side of the path were no longer barring the way. She walked past them with her head held high.

Quintus nodded to the tall youth and to the other three, each in turn, in solemn acknowledgement of their understanding. Then he followed on behind Olwen, at a stately pace. As he walked, he imagined what it would feel like if an arrow or a thrown knife were to enter through the skin and the flesh of his back, between his ribs and into his viscera. His lungs. His heart.

Neither spoke for some time. Quintus felt the sweat on his back and in his armpits dry, and his heartbeat ceased its pummelling.

Olwen was the first to speak. 'Do you expect me to thank you?'

Quintus smiled. 'I expect nothing,' he said. 'I hope for everything.'

'Whatever grovelling servility you performed, you'd better not have submitted to them on my behalf.'

'I did not,' he said. 'I negotiated. I bargained.' He walked faster to keep up with her.

'What gave you that idea?' she asked.

'I did what my father would have done, I suppose.' Quintus shook his head. 'He never raised his hand to my sister or me. But he was ruthless with persuasion. In an argument, no one could beat him.'

Olwen glanced at him, walking beside her. 'You did well,' she said, and took his hand, and on they walked.

As they walked, they ate nuts Veldicca had provided them with, and blackberries they picked from brambles in passing. Olwen pointed out a fox's scat, purple-dark. 'They've been eating blackberries too,' she said.

'Will our shit be that colour?' Quintus wondered.

'No doubt. We are animals too, are we not?'

All afternoon, they trotted through forest. By a stream a beech tree had fallen, and from its horizontal branches new shoots grew straight up like lines of fence stakes. Trees and rocks alike were covered in dark green moss. Quintus and Olwen followed a hollowed way that soil and leaves and rain had mulched into a funnel of mud. They trudged along through the sludge. It squelched between their toes. When they climbed out of the hollow and ran along the bank above, pigs rootled and rummaged in the undergrowth. The pigs did not scatter at the youths' approach, and Olwen said there must be a farm nearby, as the pigs were not wild.

'I love pigs,' Olwen said.

'You mean you like the taste of them?'

'No. I love swine because they eat acorns and beech mast, which are poisonous to horses. Is that not a fine thing?'

Soon the wood opened out. They heard a noise and looked around. It sounded to Olwen like the Druid who, when he meditated, hummed to himself in a steady drone. She felt Quintus touch her arm. His head was upturned and he faced the sky, eyes shielded with his left hand. She followed his gaze. A large bird, all bone, cruised across the firmament.

Quintus said that what drifted high up there resembled a Christian cross. A new religion. Those adherents who had appeared in Ephesus spoke of miracles performed by their Christ. They spoke of signs and prophecies. No one he knew had taken them seriously. Perhaps this was a miraculous sign, a declaration of their superior magic. He could not fathom why it made a sound, or what the sound might mean. It reminded him of the beehives the slave Gallio had tended in his master's garden. Now it faded.

They could no longer hear it, but they continued watching the object in its stately progress across the sky.

'The bird has a light on each wing,' Olwen said, 'like the will-o'-the-wisps in the marshes beyond Bryn Rhudd.' They watched the object grow ever smaller. 'I cannot see it any more,' Olwen said, and turned to Quintus. He still gazed upwards. 'Can you still see it?' she asked.

'Yes,' he said. Then he said, 'No,' and lowered his gaze.

'It has flown north, towards the mountains,' Olwen said. She shook her head. 'You must have very good sight. I have excellent eyes. So yours must be exceptional.'

Quintus smiled. 'Either that,' he said, 'or I am a liar.'

They found a path and followed it through a stand of poplars, whose last leaves rustled in the breeze. Then they entered a clearing.

Olwen stopped. 'There is someone behind us,' she said.

Quintus listened. 'I cannot hear anyone.'

'Neither can I,' she said. 'But he is there.'

'He?'

'He sits ahorse.' Olwen glanced around. 'Stay here. When he reaches you, tell him your kidnapper has fled.'

'Are you serious?'

'Appear confused,' she said, then turned and ran.

Quintus stood on a path with trees on one side and a stone bluff on the other, above it rough ground sloping further upwards. He watched her climb the gradient and disappear amongst the brush. Then he heard sounds, and turned in the direction from which they had come.

He beheld a horseman, who studied the ground as he walked his horse. A legionary. Then the soldier looked up and saw Quintus, and halted his mount. He cast around, and gazed again upon the boy. Then he pricked his horse and came at a slow pace towards him with his spear raised, glancing around.

Quintus held up his arms in greeting, and out in subservience. Perhaps the soldier would not kill him. Not immediately. He was lightly apparelled, with neither helmet nor armour. A scout, clearly. A tracker. Perhaps one of those they had seen in the wood but mounted now. He halted his horse two or three yards away and addressed

Quintus while still peeking nervously about to either side and even, once, behind him.

'Where is she?'

'She fled when first she heard you. Thank Jupiter you rescued me.'

'Rescued?'

'She kidnapped me.'

The soldier stared at Quintus. His contempt was palpable. The young slave who never got his hands dirty, the unofficial interpreter, the governor's favourite, knew this look well. There was no need for the legionary to conceal it. Then his expression altered. A smile, a grin, spread across his weathered face.

'I was right,' he said.

'You were?'

'That's what I told them,' the soldier said. 'Pursuing you, at night we have argued over the nature of your flight. One reckoned you who speak their language made a pact with her. Another that you struck a bargain with her father to return her intact to him, you ungrateful scum. A third fancied that you were merely foolish young lovers. But I said she needed a hostage in her flight and took the weakest of our number, who could yet run with her.'

Quintus shook his head slowly.

'The blood on her cloak?' the legionary asked. 'Celtic trickery. I guessed it.'

'I will tell them you were right,' Quintus said. 'Though it pains me to admit.'

The soldier nodded, pleased with himself. 'Many of us can fight, boy,' he said. 'None of us can make sense of the clotted speech of primitives the way you can. The Gauls. These Britons.' He ceased smiling, and frowned. 'Wait,' he said. 'Why take a hostage, then flee as soon as she requires him?'

'She took fright when she saw you,' Quintus conjectured in return.

Their discourse was interrupted. There came the sound of a rapid drumbeat. Quintus saw the soldier turn and look past the rock bluff and up to the slope above it. The sound was not a drum but running feet. Then came a greater noise, a blood-freezing scream such as Quintus had never heard. He turned too and saw Olwen sprinting down the slope, her face an ugly rictus of hatred, her mouth filled with gnashing teeth. She held her sword by the handle but upside down, the swifter to run. She reached the stone ledge and leapt off the rock, flipping the sword as she flew through the air and grasping the hilt with her other hand as well.

The legionary was slow to react. It was likely that he was a fine tracker rather than a fierce fighter. He raised his spear, but too late. Olwen landed with one foot on the rump of the soldier's horse as she raised the sword above her shoulder and swung it. The sword cut through the soldier's neck, separating his head from his shoulders. Olwen tumbled to the ground on the far side.

The horse meanwhile bucked, whether from the sudden weight upon its rump or the shock from this aerial intrusion, or both together, and shied dramatically. Seeing the hooves rear up before him Quintus jumped backwards, avoiding thereby the soldier's severed head, which landed on the ground beside the horse and rolled towards him.

The legionary's headless corpse lost all stability and flopped this way and that grotesquely upon the rearing horse, letting go the reins, one foot losing its hold in the stirrup. The horse bolted. It galloped across the clearing and disappeared around the curve of the hill. The lifeless rider fell, catching one foot in a stirrup, and was dragged along the ground.

Olwen lay down her sword and picked up the severed head. She closed her eyes and breathed deeply. Then she opened her eyes and hurled the head into the undergrowth. She collected her sword and came forward.

'We must hurry,' she said. 'They will not be far behind.' She studied Quintus. 'Why are you trembling? Are you ill?'

'You have slain another human being,' Quintus stuttered, 'with great brutality. I cannot become accustomed to it.'

'The Romans have slaughtered many. You must have seen killing.'

'At a distance,' he admitted. 'It is very different so close.'

The night was cool, and they lay close to the fire. Quintus lay beside Olwen in the darkness, listening to her relaxed breathing. She had turned on her side away from him in her sleep but somehow wriggled back towards him so her bottom pressed companionably against his groin, and thus he slept.

When he woke, Quintus rolled onto his back. Above him the sky was full of stars, ablaze in the white fire of that nocturnal firmament. Then Olwen woke too, and whispered to him that she was sorry. She should not have asked him to run with her.

Quintus said that his limbs ached, he was hungry, cold, exhausted. Yes, she had put him in mortal danger, he was almost constantly terrified. Yet happier than he had ever been. He did not understand it.

'Neither do I, my love,' Olwen whispered. 'But I will tell you another story, about a pestilence that once passed across this island. Seven in every ten people who caught the plague died of it. The elderly, those in the prime of life, youths and maidens, children. There was no pattern in who sickened and died. Men and women lost their reason, ran grief-stricken from place to place. The land was untilled, animals abandoned, even the trees and the waters weakened.

'But some kept their wits, and were brave, and sought the cause of this plague. One such was a woman by the name of Rhiannon.'

'You have told me of her before. Your grandmother.'

'Yes. Rhiannon travelled the land. She met a man who said he had seen a dragon breathing fire, and she did not believe him, for no dragons had been seen on this island for hundreds of years. Then she met a woman who said she had seen a dragon breathing fire, and she did not believe her. Then she met a child who told her of a dragon who breathed fire over his village and all the people caught the plague, and this she did believe.

'Rhiannon laid a trap for the dragon. She gathered people and they dug a deep pit on a hill not far from here. Then they wove a wide carpet and laid it over the mouth of the pit. Rhiannon cooked a sweet loaf filled with nuts and berries. The people had to make a cave into an oven to bake this loaf in, it was so large, and they placed it on the carpet. And by and by the dragon flying high overhead saw the loaf, and came down to eat it. But when it landed, the carpet gave way and the dragon plummeted with the carpet and the cake into the deep pit.

'Then the people rushed to fill in the pit and bury the dragon beneath a great weight of soil and stone. Rhiannon said that as long as that dragon stayed buried in the earth, no more plague would come to the island of Britannia.' Olwen kissed Quintus. 'And you,' she whispered. 'I want to know how your life in Ephesus came to an end. You were the son of a wealthy family. How did you become a slave?'

Quintus took a deep breath, and sighed. 'My father overstretched himself. A ship from Rome full of amber and glass, gold and silver, went down in a storm. A caravan of spices and silk from the east never arrived. He'd secured lower prices by paying in advance. Our warehouse was empty. His debts were called in. He had nothing to sell. When it came, our ruin happened so fast.'

Olwen shook her head. 'I do not understand these things of which you speak, my love, but I understand the word ruin. No house stands forever.'

'Our house was no longer ours,' he agreed. 'Nor our possessions. Our servants.'

'You had slaves yourself?'

'In the house, yes. They were taken.'

Quintus stopped speaking. Olwen placed a hand on his shoulder. After a while longer she said, 'What happened then?'

'My father was executed, by the garrotte. As an example, you see? The city functioned on trade. A merchant who took credit and failed to pay it back had to be punished.'

'Your mother?'

'My mother and sister were sold into slavery. They disappeared.'

'And you?'

'I was known to have an ear for languages. The chief debtor was the wealthiest man in Ephesus. He bestowed gifts on those he thought might be useful, gave them as a fisherman baits his hook. I believe he detected imperial ambition in his friend Frontinus, and so gave me to my master.'

'Frontinus took you to Rome?'

Quintus nodded. 'I had been set to become a citizen of Ephesus. Instead I became a slave, in Rome and then wherever my master took me. I became a nobody. A citizen of nowhere.'

Quintus lay watching the fire. The night was cold, there was barely any wind, but the embers glowed red, then died to black, then glowed red again. It was as if there were a beast out there in the darkness, out of sight but close, silently inhaling and exhaling, its breath like slow bellows, animating their fire. He closed his eyes and drifted into sleep.

9

IN the night he dreamed that as they slept a myriad of creatures wandered around them. In the darkness he could not see them. Some stopped and studied Quintus and Olwen where they lay, sniffed their scent, listened to their breathing, then ambled off.

In the morning there was frost on their blankets, their hair, the ground. And all around were prints of tiny feet, of birds and small animals, and some larger paws, dinted in the white.

Their footsteps crunched and crackled on the grass. Silken filaments hung from bare branches, remnant threads of cobwebs that would surely have been invisible had not tiny droplets of dew condensed on them and frozen. Icicles hung from the trees.

As Olwen and Quintus walked the chill and stiffness out of their muscles, stars blinked out one by one in the dark sky above and the world became increasingly visible. An orange glow suggested itself in the east behind them. Before them, on the western horizon, and indeed all around, was a band of sheer blue. Upon it lay a pink strip, merging into pale blue above, as if the sun were teasing the sky before it rose into view.

In a meadow, white gulls scoured the turf and pecked at it like chickens for grubs or mites. Where the grass was longer it was rimed white with frost.

Flocks of starlings flew above them with a massed whisper of wings. They disappeared but must have wheeled around in great wide circles, for they came again, hundreds, thousands of them in a stretchy, gauzy flock. Quintus wondered how they avoided hitting each other. Olwen said they probably did, if only he could be bothered to watch more closely.

Just before the sun emerged, the light across all the heavens was blue, indigo, ultramarine, and other colours Quintus knew no name for. The light became charged and everything that was illuminated – trees, grass, each other – seemed to give notice of the imminent appearance of something wondrous. The world held its breath. The light foretold the birth of a new morning. Then the sun rose behind them and they walked on into the newborn world.

The temperature rose. From trees, water dripped off dangling icicles. They came to a small farm in a dark valley. Olwen knocked on the door of the roundhouse. A woman opened it.

'We are hungry,' Olwen said. 'We are travelling.'

'Please,' the woman said, gesturing inside with a sweep of her arm. 'Enter my house.'

They sat. The woman fussed around her fire, and came to them with wooden bowls of porridge made with oats and goat milk. When they had eaten, they rose to leave, but first Olwen gave the woman a coin. The woman pressed upon them oat cakes for their journey. 'Hurry,' she said.

They crossed scrubby country. Small wild boar rootled amongst the undergrowth. Hazels were hung with catkins. Nests of mistletoe were high up in the leafless trees. A thrush bashed snails on a stone to break their shells and eat them.

They climbed onto wet upland bog. Snipe flew overhead, their wings in flight sounding like drums beating in the sky. They saw a buzzard mobbed by three crows. The buzzard glided around and the corvids harassed it, flying above it and dropping onto it, perhaps even nipping at it, they were so close. Quintus could not understand what he saw. Surely the bird of prey could kill a crow in a second with its talons.

'Are the crows protecting their young?' he asked.

'Their young will have long flown the nest,' Olwen said. 'I do not know why they do that. It's like farmers attacking a warrior. It makes no sense to me.'

Olwen trotted ahead. Quintus followed in her footsteps. He saw her step on a stone which flipped onto its side beneath her. Perhaps it had been finely balanced on a smaller stone beneath. Olwen's leg buckled sideways at the ankle. She staggered, then keeled over, landing in soft undergrowth. Olwen frowned and raised herself on to her elbows. She looked around, as if to discover who had dealt her this underhand blow. She looked up at Quintus.

'I am glad,' she said, 'you found that amusing, slave boy.'

'Such a small stone,' he said, nodding towards the culprit, 'brought down such a big girl.'

'Do you want me to wipe that grin off your face?' she asked.

'If you like, I'll show you what it looked like from behind, so you can see a witness couldn't help but laugh.'

He saw the anger within her spark in her eyes. She sprang to her feet, but when she put weight on her left foot she screamed and fell back to the ground.

'What is it?' Quintus said, and came forward. He knelt beside her. 'What's wrong, my love?' He realised all at once – too late – that it was probably a ruse. She would grab him. But she did not.

Olwen grimaced. 'It's my ankle.'

'You've turned it.'

'Sweet mother of mercy,' she cursed.

He helped her up. They ascertained that she was unable to walk. There were two options. She could hop, or he could be her bearer.

Quintus carried Olwen piggyback. At first she was a little lighter than he had expected, but she was a dead weight and became progressively heavier with each step he took.

'I wonder how good they are at stalking,' Olwen said, her mouth close to his ear. 'Will they realise you're carrying me, or will they think we split up?'

'They'll presume I'm on my own, and choose to ignore me,' Quintus said.

'Do you believe so?' she asked.

'Not really,' he admitted.

'You know they're going to catch up with us,' Olwen said. She added that she did not know where she was. They had now gone beyond all the territory she had ever explored.

They descended from the moor and followed a path beside a stream, and entered a region of steep wooded ravines, of confluent brooks and streams. The land in between was all marsh and mud. Quintus took to a rindle that ran shallow and clear over brown stones. The barks of the trees that grew tight together on either bank were green, and the boulders by the stream were covered in moss. The insistent sound of running water lapped at their ears.

Quintus paused to rest on a small island midstream. When they resumed, he stepped down into the water. Olwen stood on a rock, ready to climb onto his back. Instead he turned to face her, leaned forward and put his right arm around her legs. 'Fall onto my shoulder,' he said.

Olwen hesitated.

He lifted her legs and hoisted her onto his right shoulder. 'Put your right arm around my neck.'

This time Olwen obeyed.

'A bit further,' Quintus said, then he took hold of her wrist with his right hand. 'Good,' he said. He jiggled her body across him. 'This feels more comfortable.'

'For you, perhaps,' Olwen replied.

'For the moment, anyhow,' he affirmed, and set off upstream.

They took a further tributary off to the left. The wood closed in on either side, the trees reaching out and hanging over the water, stretching to entwine with each other across the stream. The branches blocked out light. The water ran cold and swift. Quintus made slow progress in the gloom.

'You've captured yourself a prize there, look you,' a voice proclaimed. 'But you're lost, I'd say.'

Quintus stopped. He could feel Olwen's body over his shoulders tense, helpless upon him. He looked around.

'We've not seen a human being in this creek for years.'

The voice came from the right-hand bank. Quintus peered at the trees close-packed together. All was darkness within the wood. Then a figure emerged, taking a step forward into the murky light.

The man wore animal furs on his body, his legs, his head. His face was half-covered in a scraggly grey beard.

'Let me down,' Olwen hissed.

The man's eyes were blue. 'Is it help you need there?' he asked. He seemed some kind of woodland creature. He was short and plump like a small bear.

Quintus could not see a weapon. 'Yes,' he said. 'We do.'

Olwen wriggled. 'Will you let me down?' she demanded.

Quintus relaxed his grip on her wrist, wrapped his free left arm awkwardly around her legs and eased her off his shoulder. She slid into the water, resting on the riverbed on her right leg. Grasping hold of him, she turned, hopping on her good foot, to face the stranger.

'Are you injured, lass?' he asked.

'No, I always make my servant carry me across the country,' she replied. She shook her head, as if to free it of its bad temper. 'Yes, of course I am.'

'Come with me,' the man suggested. 'Have my wife take a look at you.'

The man stepped back and disappeared again. Olwen climbed onto Quintus's back and they clambered out of the creek and into the wood. There was no path, but the man had waited for them. He pushed branches aside and, a way cleared, they stayed close and followed him.

The man's wife was of a similar stature, and wore the same fur clothes. Her name was Ria. Her husband was called Aesu. Their home was a ramshackle wooden construction of no obvious design. Perhaps a small roundhouse built too hurriedly. An area of the ground inside was covered in small animal skins, sewn together, for sleeping or sitting, and the woman bade Olwen lie on them while she examined her foot. The ankle was swollen. The woman squeezed and bent it, much to Olwen's discomfort. She bit the inside of her cheeks, eyes closed, grimacing, and made no sound.

'I can't be sure,' Ria said, 'but I don't feel any bones broken. It's badly sprained, for sure. I'll rub in some beaver grease.'

'Beaver grease?' Quintus asked.

'The best healer there is.'

The couple gave their guests roasted beaver meat with unleavened bread. They drank a hot drink, some kind of herb or berry infusion, from crude clay goblets. There were only two of each item of crockery, so each couple shared, and there were no utensils: they ate with their fingers. Midway through the meal Ria told her husband to give them a spoon. 'Of course,' he said, surprised, seemingly reminded of a long-forgotten implement. There were small knives, too, fashioned from beaver's teeth.

Ria gave each of the young pair what she proclaimed was the real delicacy, the tail of the beaver, also roasted.

Quintus expressed his and Olwen's gratitude and appreciation.

'She can cook beaver meat any way you care to mention,' Aesu said. 'Any part of the creature.'

His wife bowed and shook her head modestly, apologising for being unable to offer them the raw liver, which she and her husband had already consumed when they butchered the creature, shortly before their guests' appearance.

'We don't eat the feet, do we, my love?' she said. 'I believe some people do.'

That night all slept close together on the fur pelts, with more covering them for warmth. Beavers were clearly small animals, for the quilts were sewn from many patches. There emanated from the host couple an animal smell, whether from their clothing or themselves Quintus could not tell. It was not disagreeable. He woke intermittently, and found the aroma had increased with their mutual warmth.

———

In the morning Ria rubbed more grease into Olwen's swollen ankle.

'We cannot stay,' Olwen said, wincing.

'You cannot walk,' the woman told her. 'Perhaps tomorrow you will be able to.'

Smoke from the fire in the middle of their rickety wooden dwelling rose and dispersed through countless gaps in the ceiling, which seemed to be of mud plus sticks and leaves and similar debris. Hanging on leather string from the ceiling laths were various pouches, bark caskets and sundry items. Aesu explained that these were mostly slabs of meat, smoking and drying. He showed them a mixture his talented wife had invented of meat, grease and berries. 'Feeds us through the seasons,' he said. There were also single sticks hung that put Quintus in mind of some musical instrument. Did each sound a different note when struck? Aesu smiled and shook his head. 'Bits of wood beavers have chewed,' he said. 'To sharpen their teeth. The sticks will bring me luck in hunting them.'

'We have to leave,' Olwen said.

'Someone is after you?' Ria asked.

Olwen nodded.

'To look at you, I am not surprised. You must each come from very different tribes. One of them or perhaps both are unhappy with your union. Am I right?'

Olwen nodded again. 'Which tribe do you two belong to?' she asked.

'None,' the man interjected.

'Each belongs to his or her own tribe,' Olwen said. 'Whether kings or slaves or any in between.'

'We are outlaws,' Aesu said.

'You were expelled?' Olwen asked.

'Not really,' Ria replied. She gestured to her husband. 'He cannot live with other people. He gets irritated by their habits. Their behaviour. Irascible. Then he causes trouble.'

Quintus thought this unlikely, the man was so affable.

As if reading his mind, Ria continued, 'Oh, he's all right now. He'll be charming for two days. Even three. He likes you. But stay a day too long, you'll see another side of him.'

Aesu listened to this appraisal of his personality with equanimity.

'You do not have this effect on him?' Olwen asked.

'She has saved me from myself,' Aesu said. Then he leaned towards his wife, grabbed her and rolled over with her on the fur rugs. She burst out laughing, while telling him to take his hands off her. 'I love her,' Aesu said. 'I cannot help myself, my darling beaver, can I?'

Quintus did not think he had ever seen two greyheads gambolling like small children. He glanced at Olwen, who caught his eye. She winked at him.

———

Aesu assured Olwen and Quintus that no pursuers would find them here. It was a hidden place. They must stay. Olwen said they had nothing to give them. Aesu said Quintus could assist him today, and learn how to trap beavers. Who knows how useful such a skill might one day be to them?

Beaver fur, Aesu explained, is the most waterproof there is. He gave Quintus such clothing to wear. Trousers and jerkin. 'They are mammals, but they spend most of their lives in water,' Aesu added.

Aesu led Quintus out of their clearing. He could see no path. As before, they seemed to be surrounded by a solid barrier of small close-growing trees, whose branches were intertwined with those of their neighbours. Yet Aesu proceeded, on delicate little steps that left no imprint, into this impenetrable wall, and was swallowed by it. Quintus followed.

'This is why you are safe here. We have created our own secret paths through these woods. No one else could find them. The only way into our domain is along the network of watercourses, and who would even think to enter those?'

Beside a creek Aesu had hewn a run-off and dug a pool. In this pool were two nets made of sinew and hide twisted together, which he had soaked overnight in water and alder bark to remove his human scent. He found a stick and hooked the nets out of the water, passing one to Quintus, who found a broken branch and carried it likewise.

They splashed up the creek as far as a dam. Beavers had constructed it from sticks and mud. Aesu pointed further upstream, to a pile of wood. The beavers' lodge.

As he studied the untidy construction, with its mud and leaf roof, Quintus saw how similar it was to the trapper couple's house. They had built themselves just such a lodge.

'See how the water's backed up,' Aesu said. 'The beavers go in and out of their lodge underwater. They need the deep water to be safe from their predators. Wolf, fox, lynx.'

'Clever.'

'Oh yes. Clever creatures, beavers.'

Quintus watched as Aesu positioned the traps in the water by the bank, holding them in place by rough stakes he drove into the stream bed. Then he took a small wooden tub from his pocket and flipped the lid. He poked a stick inside and brought it out with the tip covered in a jellylike substance. This he smeared onto the top of the net above the surface of the water.

Quintus asked what it was.

'Sniff it,' Aesu whispered, passing over the tub.

Quintus raised it to his nose and blanched. It smelled of leather, urine, musk. 'Where did you get this from?' he asked.

The trapper grinned and did not answer. He attached a pole to each of the nets. At the end of each pole he hung a necklace of what he said were sheep's hooves. Then they backed away, into the wood. Aesu walked on tiptoe, keeping his voice low. 'I swear that if I'm not careful they can feel vibrations from my footsteps going from the land through the water.'

'Why are you whispering?' Quintus asked.

'I don't believe their hearing is much good, but I could be wrong, see?' Aesu found a pocket of space between trees close to the bank and sat on a log. 'Now we wait,' he said softly. He took a stone from his pocket along with a shard of bone, and began to rub the bone with the rough stone.

'How long do you expect we'll need to wait?' Quintus asked.

Aesu shrugged. 'You never know with beavers,' he said.

Quintus watched Aesu painstakingly sharpen the bone shard. He looked around. Leaning against the trunk of a tree were five or six long sticks. No, spears. With bone spearheads. Aesu must have put them here in readiness. Quintus wished he had something to do.

Then Aesu spoke again. 'Beavers are interesting creatures,' he said. 'A male and a female live together, monogamous. They patrol their territory and mark it together, using a mixture of what you sniffed just now and their own piss. They bring up their young together. The kits can

156

swim soon after birth. This year's mostly stay inside the lodge. Last year's explore the pond. Their parents will expel them in the spring, before the next lot is born. They'll go off, build a lodge and a dam of their own, maybe. Look for a mate.'

Quintus asked how many there were in a litter.

'It varies,' the trapper said. 'Five, six.' He spoke quietly, but now he had started he did not stop. He told Quintus more of the beaver's habits and eccentricities: 'The male lives in the lodge with the rest of his colony, but sometimes he goes off and stays in tunnels or dens in the riverbank. I've not yet figured out why.'

Aesu told Quintus that there were many streams and tributaries in this sheltered, secret terrain, with a number of beaver colonies, and he was the only trapper. He caught one animal a day, every day of the year. 'They roam their territory. When they come across the scent of another beaver I believe they can tell whether it's from a neighbour or some wandering rival. They'll be friendly to a neighbour, which could be one of their offspring, but get aggressive with an outsider.' He said that as a species beavers were generally nocturnal but that those here, perhaps habituated to the gloom, ventured out at all times of the day or night.

At that moment there came a sound of jiggling or clacking. Aesu leapt to his feet, stuffing his tools back into a pocket, grasped hold of a spear, and ran towards the pool. Quintus grabbed a spear and followed.

The sound had come from the sheep's hooves, a rattle. The trapper jumped down into the water, lifted one of the leather cages and flung it up on the bank. He drew back the spear. But he did not throw or strike it at the animal thrashing about. Instead, he waited. Quintus did not know why. Then Aesu lowered the spear, shaking his head. 'A youngster,' he said. He climbed up onto the bank and lifted the net into the air with its opening downward so the beaver tumbled out onto the ground. It took a swift look around, then scrabbled to the water and swam away.

Aesu carried the leather net back to their waiting place, took his seat upon the log and soon resumed sharpening his bone spearhead. Before long he resumed also his peroration on the nature of beavers.

'Never eat the head,' he said, solemnly, in case Quintus was considering imminently performing just such an act. 'You must return the head to the water, so the colony can say farewell in their fashion. Even though by then the dead one will have moved on.'

'Where to?' Quintus asked.

'Into some other animal, of course,' Aesu replied.

'Another beaver?'

'Perhaps. Or different. A bird. A fish!' This last suggestion amused the trapper, and he chuckled.

'It would be sad to come back as the animal you ate before,' Quintus mused.

'Beavers don't eat fish!' Aesu exclaimed. 'A lot of fools imagine they do, swimming about with those teeth of theirs, when all they eat is tree bark and the odd plant. The trouble with people is that they make assumptions without knowing the facts. Are they lazy? Incurious? Or just plain—'

The trapper was interrupted by the rattle of the sheep's hooves. He leapt up as before. Quintus followed and watched Aesu jump into the creek and manhandle the net onto the bank. He drew back the spear and this time thrust it into the body of the creature within. Its death throes were brief. It ceased struggling and became limp, lifeless, almost at once. Aesu climbed out. He put his foot on the beaver's body in the net and carefully worked the spear loose. He raised the net. The dead animal flopped onto the ground.

Aesu passed the net to Quintus. 'Get the other one,' he said. 'We'll go back to camp now.' He lifted the beaver by two of its webbed feet, waited for Quintus to retrieve the first leather net, then led the way.

Outside their lodge the beaver-trapping couple had set up a workstation. Between two slender tree trunks and several of its branches was a frame. The hide of the beaver Aesu had caught the day before was stretched across it, sewn in place, drying.

Nearby was a rough wooden surface on which the woman, Ria, placed the dead beaver her husband had just caught. First they requested forgiveness from the animal. They had no choice. Then Aesu closed its eyes, so it could not see what was about to be done to its body. Ria sharpened a bone-handled knife on a stone. Olwen hobbled out of the lodge to watch, leaning against Quintus.

Ria cut off the beaver's feet and tail. She laid it on its back and slit the hide from tail to lip. Then she slid the knife under the skin on one side and cut through the subcutaneous fat, lifting the skin with her free hand as she did so.

Aesu had unstitched the dried pelt from the frame. He threw it up onto the roof of the lodge, then joined the others to watch his wife at her work, intermittently telling their guests what she was doing, for their education and to share with them his appreciation of her skill. He broke off to set an iron pot full of water to boil on the fire inside the lodge, adding to it strips of bark he told them came from an oak tree.

When she reached the legs, Ria did not cut the skin but pulled the legs carefully up while unrolling the pelt off them. Then she turned the beaver over and continued to cut the fat and ease the pelt off its back. When this was done she cut around the head and pulled the skin free.

Aesu stepped forward and took the skinned carcass and placed it at the end of the wooden surface, closest to the lodge, and began to butcher it with his own sharp knife. Ria meanwhile cleaned or fleshed the hide, scraping off what remained of the fat into a wooden tub.

'She's as good a hide cleaner as you'll find anywhere,' Aesu said, nodding towards his wife. 'She'll not rip the skin, and once she's repaired any bite wounds you can hardly tell they were there.'

'Show them the glands,' Ria said.

Aesu obediently invited Olwen and Quintus to step nearer, and pointed out the sacs in its groin, around which she had worked carefully. 'These are what hold the yellow exudate you smelled earlier,' he told Quintus.

The trapper butchered the beaver, swiftly and with dexterity. The flesh he put to one side, small steaks and fillets, viscera on the other. He speared a dollop of dark meat on the tip of his knife and held it out to Olwen. 'Raw liver,' he said. 'Nothing better for whatever ails you.'

Once Ria had fleshed the pelt, Aesu fetched the iron pot from the lodge. The water had become dark brown, almost black, with tannin. He poured a little onto the hairless side of the pelt and with an old piece of leather began to rub it into the hide.

'You work hard,' Olwen observed. 'Both of you.'

'What else would we do?' Ria asked.

'We do what we choose to do,' Aesu emphasised. 'There's no swine tells us to do it.'

'You see what I mean? He's an awkward old sod.'

'She's the one who takes the pelts to the new port downriver,' Aesu told them. 'Twice a year. She's better at bartering than me.'

'What do you trade them for?' Olwen asked.

'Flour. A pot, a knife. An amphora of Roman wine.'

'Or Spanish wine,' Aesu said. 'She likes Spanish wine.'

Quintus accompanied Aesu when he carried the beaver's head back to where they had trapped the animal, and tossed it into the pool above the dam. It was full dark when they returned to the lodge. They ate the same food as the night before, and slept again burrowed under the warm rugs.

In the night Quintus woke to find the couple in murmured conversation. He wondered whether one or both were somewhat deaf, for they spoke in whispers but loudly.

'We never had kits of our own,' Aesu said.

'They can't stay,' Ria hissed.

'I'll be good. I will.'

'There are people after them. We're safe here. They put us in danger. They have to leave.'

'One more day,' Aesu begged. 'Give me that. I like them.'

———

The next morning was cold and damp and gloomy. Ria massaged grease into Olwen's ankle, whose swelling was miraculously reduced. 'Your ankle is healed, is it not?' Ria asked.

'Yes. Almost.'

Quintus went with Aesu to a different dam on another creek. Perhaps this semiaquatic realm of waterways and ponds in amongst the marshy woods had been engineered by beavers' labours. They caught and killed an adult, and carried it back to the lodge. Ria sharpened her knife to skin it as she had the one on the previous day. Aesu said he needed to take the nets to another pool to soak them and would return shortly. Quintus offered to go with him, but Aesu said it was not far. It would take him no time at all. 'Stay with the women, here.'

Olwen asked Ria if she could help in any way.

'Can you walk?'

Olwen rested her weight on the ground. She grinned at Quintus. 'This woman is a mender,' she said. 'A witch.'

'Then go. Leave. If you wish to help.'

Quintus saw Olwen struggle to contain herself. Would gratitude allow her to let a commoner, an outlaw, speak to her in this way?

They heard the rustle of branches and turned to glimpse movement in the trees. Aesu appeared in the clearing. He staggered forward in a comical manner, bringing to mind the way he had wrestled with his wife on the rugs on their first evening. He put his arms out to either side, to keep his balance, but could not stop himself from stepping from one side to the other. Back. Forward. As if the ground were bucking beneath him.

Aesu opened his mouth to speak, but instead of words came blood. Now Quintus saw the head of a spear or arrow protruding through the fur jerkin Aesu wore, out of his belly. The trapper sank to his knees.

It was not a comedy. None spoke, nor moved, but only stared at Aesu, who gazed up at them with a despairing look and then fell forward.

Ria did not tend to her husband but turned and dashed into the lodge. Quintus and Olwen followed, to find her tossing tools and other items into a leather bag. They gathered their weapons. She said nothing to them but ran back out of the lodge and across the clearing on the opposite side from which Aesu had just entered. She disappeared into the trees. Quintus grabbed Olwen's hand and said, 'Come on,' and ran after her.

Ria did not run fast. She trotted like her husband, on tiptoe, on her short legs, and they were able to keep up with her as she traversed an invisible path between the trees.

Quintus asked Olwen over his shoulder if her ankle was all right. Was she able to run?

'I feel it,' she said. 'But it's not painful.'

They ran on. Ria was slow, but she had stamina. Suddenly she stopped. Quintus thought perhaps she had heard something, and pricked up his ears, but could hear nothing. It seemed to him that perhaps the dim murk before them had glimmers of light. Ria stepped forward and lifted a branch aside. Then another. They had reached the edge of the woods. The beaver trappers' strange domain. Ria scanned the vista. Quintus and Olwen pressed close around her, and looked out. Before them lay the open country of the Preseli Hills.

'Go ahead,' she said. 'West. The ocean is there. The new port. You may find a trader who can give you passage. Two, three days' walk. A day's run.'

'Where will you go?' Olwen asked.

'Never you mind.'

'I'm sorry,' Quintus said. 'We're so sorry.'

Ria shook her head. She stepped forward and set off walking south.

They trotted west, towards the setting sun. They passed a small tree alive with sparrows, a flock roosting. As Olwen and Quintus passed, the birds ceased squabbling and fell silent. There were snowdrops in the grass.

Outside of that sheltered watery realm the temperature was lower and the air made still colder by the wind. Their footsteps rustled frozen, brittle leaves. Trees moaned and groaned against each other. The sky was filled by a spreading bruise of dark purple cloud.

The first snow was more like hail, hard gobbets of ice hurled at their faces, stinging their skin. It thickened and softened, and the flakes settled as they landed on the cold ground. At first they could not see because they had to close their eyes and stoop into the blizzard, then even if they looked up there was nothing to see except for swirling white snowflakes. It was as if they were bottled inside some receptacle not much larger than themselves and a whimsical god was shaking it. Perhaps two such gods were tossing it one to the other.

The wind whistled and grunted and shuddered in the trees even as the snow muffled all other sounds. Olwen grabbed Quintus's hand. 'We need shelter,' she yelled, though she did not know if he could hear her. If they were lucky they might find an ancient tree under whose roots they could den up as bears do. Curl up together, their breathing lull, heartbeats slow, and doze beneath the winter storm.

They were luckier. Olwen understood afterwards from the crooked window of grey light that a top corner of the burial chamber must have fallen in and the wind barrelled through the hole and blown the entrance stone askew. It was the only explanation for what appeared before them out of the tempest, the mound already deep in snow but the entrance beckoning. They stepped down into a crypt.

There must have been other, tiny holes, found by small birds that had built their nests in there. These nests were either intact on a shelf or niche, or the twigs had scattered on the floor of the dolmen, but all were dry and made perfect kindling. They built a fire and warmed themselves, and then they made a torch and looked around the tomb. It had a central passage into the circular chamber. All around the walls were separate cubicles divided with slate partitions. In each were the bones of a single occupant, curled up like a babe, Olwen said. A babe each in its own womb.

The skeletons wore the clothes that had adorned them in the fullness of their fleshly lives. Some were frayed and turning to dust, but on others the material was brightly dyed and sturdy as if the wearers had been sepulchred but days before. One skull had some hair still. Two or three were very small. All were surrounded by possessions. A flint knife, a stone axe. Bowls, cups, plates. Some had jewellery – a simple bracelet, an armlet, a ring – circled loose around their bones.

One was much like the next, but Olwen and Quintus studied each one, appalled, spellbound. There were twelve skeletons. Two cubicles were vacant.

They laid their blankets on the ground beside the fire. They had nothing to eat.

'Did you notice whether any had been given food for their journey to the other world?' Quintus asked.

'You would steal from them?'

'My stomach rumbles.'

There were some wooden objects in the catacomb that seemed to have been placed as headrests or footstools, and these burned better than the birds' twigs. Olwen hoped the departed would forgive them.

They could no longer hear the wind. Outside the snow fell silently, and they made love amongst the dead.

Afterwards, as they lay together, Quintus asked Olwen if she had another story.

'No,' she said. 'No more. There are, but I cannot remember them. I have something else to tell you.'

Quintus waited for her to speak.

'I think I am pregnant, my love.'

'Do you know you are?'

'I am almost certain.'

'Then I am very happy.'

Olwen frowned. 'I won't be a warrior, how could I be, waddling with a big belly. Will you still love me?'

'You'll always be a warrior,' he said. 'And I'll always love you.'

10

QUINTUS did not know how long they slept. He was awoken by a horrible caterwauling. It sounded like it was just outside the burial chamber. Then the utterance became a deep growl. Then a long, mournful moan. Olwen whispered in his ear that it was a lynx, her spirit animal, and to hear one now was a good sign. The lynx had kept watch over them.

Outside, the snow had melted and the air was warm. The sun was high overhead already. As they left the chamber Olwen knelt and lowered her forehead to the ground, and prayed to the spirit of the earth. She thanked it for giving them shelter, then they walked out.

They walked past primroses and daffodils. Magpies took off at their approach. The birds seemed to rotate their wings rather than flapping them. Olwen said it was all strange country to her. She had never been here, did not know the name of any hill or stream.

Their ears were brimful of birdsong. A robin defended its territory loudly from a mixed flock of tits and finches searching for specks of nourishment. High up in the topmost branches of elm trees, grey herons put the finishing touches to their nests. The messy conglomerations of sticks looked ludicrously insecure in treetops swaying in the spring wind.

They passed through a hamlet. They saw no adults, but children came out of the roundhouses and gathered about them. One invited them to eat, and they were given a breakfast of poached eggs the children said they had borrowed from gulls, lapwings, moorhens.

The children told them they knew who they were.

'You are the one who resisted the Romans,' a girl told Olwen. 'The Romans are barbarians who kill everyone in their way, but you have escaped them.'

A boy said Olwen was an outlaw, a renegade. That the Romans could not capture her. 'Look you,' he said solemnly, 'her spirit travels with her.' And they all turned to Quintus.

The children invited them to sit, and in the warm sun to take off their tunics. They brought pots of blue dye, and brushes made of feathers tied to sticks, boar bristles or horsehairs inserted into bone. Then they painted the two travellers with woad markings. They argued over whether the blue patterns looked better on Olwen's pale or Quintus's dark skin.

'Why are you smiling?' Quintus asked.

'It seems you have become one of the painted people,' Olwen said.

Two girls rubbed white lime into Quintus's curly black hair, and spiked it up.

Olwen asked how far it was to the ocean. A boy said they were very close. A girl enquired whether they could not smell the sea.

Furrowing her brow, Olwen sniffed the air. 'Is that what it is?' she said. 'I wondered.'

'Salt,' the girl explained.

Then one by one the children backed away and disappeared inside the roundhouses of the hamlet, unwilling to say farewell.

They walked on to the west, on a path through a wood. Hawthorns frothed with white blossom. The song of a mistle thrush pierced the morning air. A wren sang lustily, its broadcast out of all proportion to its diminutive form.

'So we are nearly there,' Olwen said.

Quintus took a deep breath. 'I will be relieved when we are on the ocean,' he said. 'On a trader's ship.'

'Or in a coracle,' Olwen offered.

'And even then we shall be in flight all our lives, my love.'

'Be calm, Quintus,' she told him. 'The day of our death has been foretold. We cannot change it.'

'You think so?'

'It was written in the blood of our birth. They say it is scribed on the inside of our skulls.'

'Then perhaps ours is today.'

Olwen shook her head. 'A palm reader once told my mother she would have but one daughter, and this girl would live to a great age.'

'Perhaps he was wrong.'

'My mother believed him,' Olwen said. 'Walk faster.'

Quintus realised Olwen was increasing her speed. He had to trot to keep up.

'Do not run,' she said. She gestured to her right. Quintus looked and saw, forty feet away through the trees, a small man wrapped in a thick fur coat, stumbling along on all fours. It was as if the air was thicker for him than for others, had a more turgid consistency, dense as water, and he had to shoulder his way through it. He looked like he had dropped something and was fumbling for it but had no idea where it was.

'She's just awoken,' Olwen whispered. 'She must be very hungry.'

Quintus looked again at the old man. Who turned into a bear. 'Help,' he said, though it did not emerge from his mouth, or if it did he did not know in what language.

'She's just come out of her den. Keep walking.' Olwen held Quintus's hand, and was dragging him with her. 'Her best hope is of finding the corpse of a deer that's died in the winter.'

'How?' Quintus demanded.

'She can smell meat from far away.'

'Wait, won't she smell us?'

'We're downwind of her,' Olwen told him.

'That is a relief.'

'But the wind may change. Hurry.'

Quintus wondered whether, if the bear chased them, they could run. Olwen said they would do better to scramble up a tree, for though cubs could climb, adult bears were too heavy.

Out of woodland and onto open moor they came. On the hills leafless trees, bent and twisted, clung to the unsheltered slopes by their shallow roots, having endured another wild winter of ice and blizzard.

'They bend in the wind,' Olwen said. 'The wind makes them stronger. The sinews of their branches are like those of your legs, stronger from your running, or of my arms, from pulling the bow.'

In an upland meadow Olwen heard a curlew's bubbling cry, and saw it rise from the spring grass. She was about to tell Quintus, but realised he had already seen it and was watching it in flight. Its extraordinary long beak, its swirling chequerboard wings. They paused to watch it together. It was somehow clumsy and ludicrous and beautiful all at once.

Olwen turned to Quintus. 'What is wrong, my love?' she said. 'Why do you weep?'

Quintus shook his head. 'I did not know there was so much to see in this world,' he said. 'Where my eyes would have passed over and noticed nothing. You have shown me.'

'What you see is yours,' Olwen said. 'And there is always more. Hidden beneath the surface. Behind the trees. Beyond that hill. Munatius once told me there are seven veils between man and God.'

'That may take a long time to make one's way through.'

'He said there are five more between a man and himself.' Then she raised her hand and with her fingers wiped the tears from Quintus's eyes, and embraced him.

They passed a circle of stones. The smell of salt was stronger now, and the breeze was faint but fresh. The land sloped away and Quintus said, 'There it is.'

Olwen shook her head. Before her was grassland with bracken and gorse. Beyond was nothing, deep blue emptiness, with a line along its upper rim and above it the paler blue sky.

'Water,' Quintus told her. 'Behold the ocean.'

They walked on across the grass. Wild goats grazed, and made peevish way for them.

Reaching the edge of the land, high above the sea, they gazed upon it. Olwen peered down to the sand and rocks far below. 'My knees have become soft,' she said.

Quintus took her hand and pulled her back. 'Let's find a path down to the beach,' he said.

They turned to stroll back across the grass, then stopped stock-still. Ahead of them, fifty feet away up the slope, stood five Roman soldiers. Another was mounted upon a black horse. Severus, commander of the governor's bodyguard.

Quintus squeezed Olwen's hand. 'I understand,' he said. He let go of Olwen's hand and stepped in front of her, drawing the sword of the first Roman soldier she had killed, which he had carried all this way.

'No, Quintus,' Olwen said, behind him.

'I may not be a warrior,' he said, turning back to her. 'But I wish to die before you, Olwen.'

She took him by the shoulders and turned him back to face the legionaries and the mounted centurion. 'My love,' she whispered in his ear. 'I am always with you.'

The Romans came forward slowly. Quintus raised his sword and took some steps in their direction. Then he heard footsteps behind him, running away.

Quintus turned. Olwen was no longer there. She had disappeared.

He stepped to the edge of the cliff and peered over. Her body lay misshapen on the rocks below. Quintus stared, his brain refusing to make sense of what he saw. Then he felt his arms grasped, clamped, by powerful fingers, a man on either side.

Quintus's legs would not work. The Romans dragged him, stumbling between them, down a path they found. On the beach he was bound, and slumped upon the sand. A legionary stood guard over him.

Two of the soldiers wrapped Olwen's broken body in a calfskin sheet. A third collected driftwood for a fire. Another prepared a meal.

Severus told the legionary guarding Quintus to go and find grazing for his horse. He sat on a large rock and drank from a flask he took from his bag.

'Look at you,' he said. 'Painted like a barbarian. And what has she done to your hair?' He shook his head. 'Did she think she could escape us?' he asked. 'Outrun the Roman Empire?'

Quintus did not reply. He sat, bent over, inert.

'I imagine you are surprised,' Severus said, 'to find so senior a soldier in pursuit of you. Well, I only caught up with them yesterday. I was with the legions that marched upon her father's fort.'

Quintus looked up morosely.

'The governor was made a fool of,' Severus continued. 'He tried to make peace using a marriage treaty. Now he has to impose peace with Roman arms. Exactly what we should have done from the day we landed on this island.'

Quintus bowed his head. 'When will that happen?' he mumbled.

'It has happened already.' The centurion cast around him, at the light in the sky and how it fell upon the land and the sea. 'And still happens, even as we speak,' he said. 'We have wiped them out.'

'All of them?'

'Some were spared, initially, and made to dismantle their ramparts. You should have seen the fire. I am surprised you did not, even at this distance. They dug out the banks, filled in the ditches. When I left, they were excavating a deep pit in the middle of the hill summit to bury their kin. When that is done they will be executed too and their bodies added to the pile.' He looked thoughtful. 'I suppose it will have to be our soldiers who fill in their grave.'

The legionary who had cooked a stew brought a bowl to Severus. 'Give the slave one too,' he said.

'How will he eat it?' the cook asked.

'Cut him loose, of course.'

'He may run, sir.'

Severus laughed. 'Where is there to run to?'

After he had served the two legionaries who sat on the sand, leaning against boulders a little closer to the sea, the cook brought Quintus a bowl of stew and handed him a spoon with which to eat it.

'In a short time, a year, perhaps two, there will be no evidence,' Severus continued. 'Every last trace obliterated. She will not have existed, nor her father, nor her people. The very name of their tribe will be erased. The governor will write his account with no mention of them. Their only presence will be their absence.' This amused the centurion, and he chuckled at his own wit. 'Travellers will cross that hill and never know that one of the most powerful tribes in this land of barbarians resided there. If in a thousand, two thousand years, some fool digging there for gold finds a rusted brooch, human bones, it will mean nothing to them.'

'Have you massacred farmers too?' Quintus asked.

Severus looked at him as if he was simple. 'Of course not,' he said. 'Why would we?'

'And me? Will you not put me out of my misery, Severus? Are you to take me back just so my master can watch me being throttled?'

The centurion laughed. 'Why would he want you dead? He does not blame you for being taken by that she-devil and her people. He will be surprised if I tell him there were none, only the girl alone. But I fancy I will not, Quintus. He has a soft spot for you. We all know that. He preferred your skin to hers, let us say.'

'He never touched me, Severus, these years his slave.'

Severus nodded. 'So, Frontinus does not need to touch another's flesh. He takes all he wants with his eyes. Anyhow, he needs a good interpreter. That senile old fool Appius gets these foreign tongues mangled in his mouth. The governor will keep you until he finds another one, and where will that be?'

'And then I will be strangled, I suppose.'

The centurion shrugged. It meant nothing to him one way or another. He stood up. 'You're a slave, Quintus,' he said, without spite, and strolled over to the cook, carrying his bowl. He put it down, then ambled towards the cliff face, where he lifted his tunic to take a piss.

Quintus sprang to his feet, and had bolted between the two sitting soldiers before they could react. They jumped up and chased after him, yelling to the others. Quintus sprinted towards the sea. There was no Roman now between him and the water. The tide was out, the sea was a long way away across the sand, which gave him time to open up distance between him and his pursuers. For he was fast, and he could run forever.

Severus finished urinating in a state of infuriated agitation. He would have stopped the act, but he was not a young man any longer and he had heard that stopping yourself midstream could damage a man's waterworks. 'Get your bow!' he shouted as he peed.

The fifth legionary had begun to race after his comrades, but heard the order and turned back. He hurried to where they had stowed their weapons, grabbed a bow and a quiver of arrows, and ran off.

Severus was exasperated. 'Get me my horse!' he yelled at the cook.

Quintus ran as he had never run before. The dark sand was wet and firm and he barely touched it but flew across the surface. He hared through the shallows then, as the cold water deepened, waded, slowing down. Glancing over his shoulder, he saw the two soldiers far away. A third carried a bow. In the distance was a figure mounted on a horse, gesticulating wildly.

As the water reached his waist, Quintus dived forward.

He swam as far and as fast as he could without breathing. When he needed air, he rolled over almost onto his back and looked to the shore as he took in great gulps.

He saw an arrow come arching towards him and land in the water close by. Soon another arrow came, but it fell short. Quintus saw the horseman turning his horse in the shallows, furious. Then he rolled onto his front, and swam further on, into the vast ocean before him.

The air was warm but the water was cold, colder than it had been in the river when they first began their flight across the country. As he proceeded, Quintus grew increasingly tired. He understood he might not carry on much longer, but he would for as long as he was able. He decided Olwen had been right. She really was pregnant. If only it had been allowed, they would have raised the first of a new race on this island.

Teeth chattering, bone-frozen, Quintus swam on, ever slower, swallowing the cold salt water, his mind unwinding. Dreaming of Olwen's warm embrace.

And on he swam,

until at last

he sank into eternity.

AUTHOR'S NOTE

Sextus Julius Frontinus was Roman governor of Britain from AD 74 to 77. Under his command the Romans subjugated the Silures tribe in modern-day south-east Wales and the Demetae in the south-west. Frontinus built a fort in Caerleon, or Isca – one of three legionary fortresses in Britain – whose baths, barracks and amphitheatre can be visited today.

He established a string of smaller forts for auxiliary units, including one in Luentinum, by the modern village of Pumsaint, near the gold mines of Dolaucothi. Frontinus was a renowned engineer (he later restored the aqueducts of Rome and wrote a treatise on their construction), and it is likely that he began the construction of aqueducts and leets that enabled hydraulic mining at Dolaucothi. The mines too can be visited today.

According to Marcel Mauss, in Roman times the *persona* gradually became "synonymous with the true nature of the individual" but "the slave was excluded from it. *Servus non habet personam* ('a slave has no persona'). He has no personality. He does not own his body; he has no ancestors, no name, no cognomen, no goods of his own." (Wikipedia)

Olwen's family stories are filleted from Charlotte Guest's mid-nineteenth-century translations into English of the Welsh *The Mabinogion*.

There is also a Welsh legend that tells of a Roman governor and usurper of the imperial crown, Magnus Maximus (known in the legend as Macsen Wledig), who dreamed of a beautiful woman. He sent his men out to seek her. They travelled the known world and found her, Helen Luyddawc, the daughter of a Welsh king, in Caernarfon. They related the dream of their master, and requested that she accompany them, as maiden empress, to Rome. Helen, a proud Welsh princess, refused. 'If he wants me, let him come to me,' she told them. Which according to the myth he subsequently did.

ACKNOWLEDGEMENTS

Heartfelt thanks to my agent, Victoria Hobbs at AM Heath, and editor, Mark Richards at Swift Press. Special thanks to eagle-eyed copy-editor Sarah Terry, proofreader Madeleine Rogers and production editor Alex at Tetragon.

I'm indebted to Melissa Harrison, whose nature diaries (collected in *The Stubborn Light of Things*) opened my eyes. And to Iolo Williams, whose *Wild about the Wild* accompanied me on my travels across Wales.